BENEATH THE
SUGAR SKY

Center Point
Large Print

Also by Seanan McGuire and available from Center Point Large Print:

Every Heart a Doorway
Down Among the Sticks and Bones

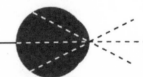

**This Large Print Book carries the
Seal of Approval of N.A.V.H.**

BENEATH THE SUGAR SKY

SEANAN McGUIRE

CENTER POINT LARGE PRINT
THORNDIKE, MAINE

For Midori,
whose doorway is waiting

This Center Point Large Print edition
is published in the year 2020 by arrangement with
Tor-Forge Books.

Copyright © 2017 Seanan McGuire.

Interior illustrations by Rovina Cai.

The text of this Large Print edition is unabridged.
In other aspects, this book may vary
from the original edition.
Printed in the United States of America
on permanent paper.
Set in 16-point Times New Roman type.

ISBN: 978-1-64358-527-7

The Library of Congress has cataloged this record
under Library of Congress Control Number: 2019954781

Sugar, flour, and cinnamon won't make
  a house a home,
So bake your walls of gingerbread and
  sweeten them with bone.
Eggs and milk and whipping cream, butter
  in the churn,
Bake our queen a castle in the hopes
  that she'll return.
            — CHILDREN'S CLAPPING
                RHYME, CONFECTION

PART I
THE EMPTY SPACES

HOME AGAIN

Children have always tumbled down rabbit holes, fallen through mirrors, been swept away by unseasonal floods or carried off by tornadoes. Children have always *traveled,* and because they are young and bright and full of contradictions, they haven't always restricted their travel to the possible. Adulthood brings limitations like gravity and linear space and the idea that bedtime is a real thing, and not an artificially imposed curfew. Adults can still tumble down rabbit holes and into enchanted wardrobes, but it happens less and less with every year they live. Maybe this is a natural consequence of living in a world where being careful is a necessary survival trait, where logic wears away the potential for something bigger and better than the obvious. Childhood melts, and flights of fancy are replaced by rules. Tornados kill people: they don't carry them off to magical worlds. Talking foxes are a sign of fever, not guides sent to start some grand adventure.

But children, ah, children. Children follow the foxes, and open the wardrobes, and peek beneath the bridge. Children climb the walls and fall down the wells and run the razor's edge of possibility until sometimes, just sometimes, the possible surrenders and shows them the way to go home.

Becoming the savior of a world of wonder and magic before you turn fourteen does not exactly teach caution, in most cases, and many of the children who fall through the cracks in the world where they were born will one day find themselves opening the wrong door, peering through the wrong keyhole, and standing right back where they started. For some, this is a blessing. For some, it is easy to put the adventures and the impossibilities of the past behind them, choosing sanity and predictability and the world that they were born to be a part of. For others . . .

For others, the lure of a world where they *fit* is too great to escape, and they will spend the rest of their lives rattling at windows and peering at locks, trying to find the way home. Trying to find the one perfect door that can take them there, despite everything, despite the unlikeliness of it all.

They can be hard for their families to understand, those returned, used-up miracle children. They sound like liars to people who have never had a doorway of their own. They sound like dreamers. They sound . . . unwell, to the charitable, and simply sick to the cruel. Something must be done.

Something like admission to Eleanor West's

Home for Wayward Children, a school for those who have gone, and come back, and hope to go again, when the wind is right, when the stars are bright, when the world remembers what it is to have mercy on the longing and the lost. There, they can be among their peers, if they can truly be said to have peers: they can be with people who understand what it is to have the door locked between themselves and home. The rules of the school are simple. Heal. Hope. And if you can, find your way back where you belong.

No solicitation. No visitors.

No quests.

1

ONE DOOR OPENS, ANOTHER IS BLOWN OFF ITS HINGES

Autumn had come to Eleanor West's Home for Wayward Children in the usual way, with changing leaves and browning grass and the constant smell of impending rain hanging heavy in the air, a seasonal promise yet to be fulfilled. The blackberry briars at the back of the field grew rich with fruit, and several students spent their afternoons with buckets in their hands, turning their fingers purple and soothing their own furious hearts.

Kade checked the seals on the windows one by one, running putty along the places where the moisture seemed likely to find a way inside, one eye on the library and the other on the sky.

Angela watched the sky too, waiting for a rainbow, ordinary shoes on her feet and enchanted shoes slung over her shoulder, laces tied in a careful, complicated knot. If the light and the water came together *just so,* if the rainbow touched down where she could reach it, she would be gone, off and running, running, running all the way home.

Christopher, whose door would open—if it ever opened for him again; if he ever got to find his way back home—on the Day of the Dead, sat in the grove of trees behind the house, playing ever more elaborate songs on his bone flute, trying to prepare for the moment of disappointment when the door failed to appear or of overwhelming elation when the Skeleton Girl called him back where he belonged.

So it was all across the school, each of the students preparing for the change of seasons in whatever way seemed the most appropriate, the most comforting, the most likely to get them through the winter. Girls who had gone to worlds defined by summer locked themselves in their rooms and wept, staring at the specter of another six months trapped in this homeland that had somehow, between one moment and the next, become a prison; others, whose worlds were places of eternal snow, of warm furs and hot fires and sweet mulled wine, rejoiced, seeing their own opportunity to find the way back opening like a flower in front of them.

Eleanor West herself, a spry ninety-seven-year-old who could pass for someone in her late sixties, and often did when she had to interact with people from outside the school, walked the halls with a carpenter's eye, watching the walls for signs of sagging, watching the ceilings for signs of rot. It was necessary to have contractors

14

in every few years to keep things solid. She hated the disruption. The children disliked pretending to be ordinary delinquents, sent away by their parents for starting fires or breaking windows, when really they had been sent away for slaying dragons and refusing to say that they hadn't. The lies seemed petty and small, and she couldn't blame them for feeling that way, although she rather thought they would change their tune if she deferred the maintenance and someone got drywall dropped on their head.

Balancing the needs of her students with the needs of the school itself was tiresome, and she yearned for the return to Nonsense and the carelessness she knew waited somewhere up ahead of her, in the golden country of the future. Like the children she called to her care, Eleanor West had been trying to go home for as long as she could remember. Unlike most of them, her struggle had been measured in decades, not months . . . and unlike most of them, she had watched dozens of travelers find their way back home while she was left standing in place, unable to follow, unable to do anything but weep.

She sometimes thought that might be the one piece of true magic this world possessed: so many children had found their way home while in her care, and yet not a single parent had accused her of wrongdoing, or attempted to launch an investigation into the disappearance of their beloved offspring. She knew their parents had loved them; she had listened to fathers weeping and held the hands of mothers who stared stoically into the shadows, unable to move, unable to process the size of their grief. But none of them had called her a killer, or demanded her school close its doors. They knew. On some level, they knew, and had known long before she came to them with the admission papers in her hands, that their children had only come back to them long enough to say goodbye.

One of the hallway doors opened, and a girl emerged, attention focused on her phone. Eleanor stopped. Collisions were unpleasant things, and should be avoided when possible. The girl turned toward her, still reading the display.

Eleanor tapped the point of her cane against the ground. The girl stopped and looked up, cheeks coloring blotchy red as she finally realized she was not alone.

"Er," she said. "Good morning, Miss West."

"Good morning, Cora," said Eleanor. "And please, it's Eleanor, if you don't mind. I may be old and getting older, but I was never a miss. More of a hit, in the places I usually roved."

Cora looked confused. That wasn't uncommon, with new students. They were still adapting to the idea of a place where people would believe them, where saying impossible things would earn them a shrug and a comment about something equally impossible, rather than a taunt or an accusation of insanity.

"Yes, ma'am," said Cora finally.

Eleanor swallowed a sigh. Cora would come around. If she didn't do it on her own, Kade would have a talk with her. He had become Eleanor's second-in-command since Lundy's death, and Eleanor would have felt bad about that—he was still only a boy, should still have been running in meadows and climbing trees, not filling out paperwork and designing curriculums—but Kade was a special case, and she couldn't deny needing the help. He would run this school one day. Better for him to start preparing now.

"How are you settling in, dear?" she asked.

Cora brightened. It was remarkable how pretty she became when she stopped looking dour and confused and a little lost. She was a short, round girl, made entirely of curves: the soft slope of breasts and belly, the gentle thickness of upper arms and thighs, the surprising delicacy of wrists and ankles. Her eyes were very blue, and her hair, long and once naturally brown, like the grass out in the yard, was now a dozen shades of green and blue, like some sort of tropical fish.

(It would turn brown again if she stayed here long enough, if she stayed dry. Eleanor had met other children who had traveled through Cora's door, and she knew, although she would never tell Cora, that on the day when the green and blue began to fade—whether that happened tomorrow or in a year—that would be when the door would be locked forever, and Cora would be shipwrecked forever on this now-foreign shore.)

"Everyone's been really nice," she said. "Kade says he knows where my world falls on the compass, and he's going to help me research other people who have gone there. Um, and Angela introduced me to all the other girls, and a few of them went to water worlds too, so we have lots to talk about."

"That's wonderful," said Eleanor, and meant it. "If there's anything you need, you'll let me know, won't you? I want all my students to be happy."

"Yes, ma'am," said Cora, the brightness fading. She bit her lip as she tucked her phone into her pocket, and said, "I have to go. Um, Nadya and I are going to the pond."

"Remind her to take a jacket, please. She gets cold easily." Eleanor stepped to the side, letting Cora hurry away. She couldn't keep up with the students anymore, and she supposed that was a good thing; the sooner she wore out, the sooner she could go home.

But oh, she was tired of getting old.

Cora hurried down the stairs, shoulders hunched slightly inward, waiting for a sneer or insult that never came. In the six weeks since she had arrived at the school, no one had called her "fat"

18

like it was another word for "monster," not even once. Kade, who served as the unofficial tailor and had a selection of clothing left behind by departing students that stretched back decades, had looked her up and down and said a number that had made her want to die a little bit inside, until she'd realized there was no judgement in his tone: he just wanted her clothes to fit.

The other students teased and fought and called each other names, but those names were always about things they'd done or places they'd gone, not about who they *were*. Nadya was missing her right arm at the elbow, and no one called her "gimp" or "cripple" or any of the other things Cora *knew* she would have been called if she'd gone to Cora's old school. It was like they had all learned to be a little kinder, or at least a little more careful about what they based their judgements on.

Cora had been fat her entire life. She had been a fat baby, and a fat toddler in swim classes, and a fat child in elementary school. Day after day, she had learned that "fat" was another way to say "worthless, ugly, waste of space, unwanted, disgusting." She had started to believe them by the time she was in third grade, because what else was she supposed to do?

Then she had fallen into the Trenches (don't think about how she got there don't think about how she might get back *don't do it*), and suddenly

19

she'd been beautiful. Suddenly she'd been strong, insulated against the bitter chill of the water, able to dive deeper and swim further than anyone else in the school. Suddenly she'd been a hero, brave and bright and beloved. And on the day when she'd been sucked into that whirlpool and dropped into her own backyard, on dry land again, no gills in her neck or fins on her feet, she had wanted to die. She had thought she could never be beautiful again.

Maybe here, though . . . maybe here she could be. Maybe here she was allowed. Everyone else was fighting toward their own sense of safety, of beauty, of belonging. Maybe she could do that, too.

Nadya was waiting on the porch, examining the nails of her hand with the calm intensity of a dam getting ready to break. She looked up at the sound of the closing door. "You're late." The ghost of a Russian accent lingered in her words and wrapped itself like waterweeds around her vowels, pale and thin as tissue paper.

"Miss West was in the hall outside my room." Cora shook her head. "I didn't think she'd be there. She's so *quiet* for being so *old*."

"She's older than she looks," said Nadya. "Kade says she's almost a hundred."

Cora frowned. "That doesn't make sense."

"Says the girl whose hair grows in green and blue all over," said Nadya. "It's a miracle your parents got you here before the beauty companies snatched you up to try to figure out the mystery of the girl with the seaweed pubes."

"Hey!" yelped Cora.

Nadya laughed and started down the porch, taking the steps two at a time, like she didn't trust them to get her where she needed to go. "I only tell the truth, because I love you, and because one day you're going to be on the front of the supermarket magazines. Right next to Tom Cruise and the Scientology aliens."

"Only because you're going to turn me in," said Cora. "Miss West told me to remind you to bring a coat."

"Miss West can bring me a coat herself if she wants me to have one so bad," said Nadya. "I don't get cold."

"No, but you *catch* colds all the time, and I guess she's tired of listening to you hack up a lung."

Nadya waved her hand dismissively. "We must suffer for our chance to return home. Now come, come, hurry. Those turtles aren't going to tip themselves."

Cora shook her head, and hurried.

Nadya was one of the school's long-timers: five years so far, from the age of eleven to the age of sixteen. There had been no sign in those five years of her doorway appearing, or of her asking her adoptive parents to take her home.

That was unusual. Everyone knew that parents could withdraw their children at any time; that all Nadya had to do was ask and she'd be able to return to the life she'd lived before . . . well, before everything.

According to everyone Cora had spoken to, most students chose to go back to their old lives after four years had passed without a doorway.

"That's when they give up," Kade had said, expression turning sad. "That's when they say, 'I can't live for a world that doesn't want me, so I guess I'd better learn to live in the world I have.'"

Not Nadya. She didn't belong to any clique or social circle, didn't have many close friends—or seem to want them—but she didn't leave, either. She went from classroom to turtle pond, from bathtub to bed, and she kept her hair perpetually wet, no matter how many colds she caught, and she never stopped watching the water for the bubbles that would mark her way back to Belyyreka, the Drowned World and the Land Beneath the Lake.

Nadya had walked up to Cora on her first day at the school, when she was standing frozen in the door of the dining hall, terrified to eat—what if they called her names?—and terrified to turn and run away—what if they made fun of her behind her back?

"You, new girl," she had said. "Angela tells me you were a mermaid. Is that so?"

Cora had sputtered and stammered and some-how signaled her agreement. Nadya had smirked and taken Cora's arm in hers.

"Good," she'd said. "I've been ordered to make more friends, and you seem to fit the bill. We damp girls have to stick together."

In the weeks since then, Nadya had been the best of friends and the worst of friends, prone to bursting into Cora's room without knocking, pestering her roommate and trying to convince Miss West to reassign one or both of them so they could room together. Miss West kept refusing, on the grounds that no one else in the school would be able to find a towel if the two girls who took the most baths were in the same place to egg each other on.

Cora had never had a friend like Nadya before. She thought she liked it. It was hard to say: the novelty of it all was still too overwhelming.

The turtle pond was a flat silver disk in the field, burnished by the sunlight, surface broken by the flat disks of the turtles themselves, sailing off to whatever strange turtle errands they had in the months before their hibernation. Nadya grabbed a stick off the ground and took off running, leaving Cora to trail behind her like a faithful balloon.

"Turtles!" Nadya howled. "Your queen returns!"

She didn't stop when she reached the edge

of the pond, but plunged gleefully onward, splashing into the shallows, breaking the perfect smoothness of the surface. Cora stopped a few feet back from the water. She preferred the ocean, preferred saltwater and the slight sting of the waves against her skin. Fresh water wasn't enough.

"Come back, turtles!" shouted Nadya. "Come back and let me love you!"

That was when the girl fell out of the sky and landed in the middle of the turtle pond with an enormous splash, sending turtles skyward, and drenching both Cora and Nadya in a wave of muddy pond water.

2 GRAVITY HAPPENS TO THE BEST OF US

The girl in the pond rose up sputtering, with algae in her hair and a very confused turtle snagged in the complicated draperies of her dress, which seemed to be the result of someone deciding to hybridize a ball gown with a wedding cake, after dyeing both of them electric pink. It also seemed to be dissolving, running down her arms in streaks, coming apart at the seams. She was going to be naked soon.

The girl in the pond didn't seem to notice, or maybe she just didn't care. She wiped water and dissolving dress out of her eyes, flicking them to the side, and cast wildly about until she spotted Cora and Nadya standing on the shore, mouths open, gaping at her.

"You!" she yelled, pointing in their direction. "Take me to your leader!"

Cora's mouth shut with a snap. Nadya continued to gawk. Both of them had traveled to places where the rules were different—Cora to a world of beautiful Reason, Nadya to a world of impeccable Logic. None of this had prepared them for women who dropped out of the sky in a shower of turtles and started yelling, especially not here, in a world they both thought of as tragically predictable and dull.

Cora recovered first. "Do you mean Miss Eleanor?" she asked. Relief followed the question. Yes. The girl—she looked to be about seventeen—would want to talk to Miss Eleanor. Maybe she was a new student, and this was how admissions worked mid-term.

"No," said the girl sullenly, and crossed her arms, dislodging the turtle on her shoulder. It fell back to the pond with a resounding *plop*. "I mean my mother. She's in charge at home, so she must be in charge here. It's only"—her lip curled, and she spat out her next word like it tasted bad— *"logical."*

"What's your mother's name?" asked Cora.

"Onishi Sumi," said the girl.

Nadya finally shook off her shock. "That's not possible," she said, glaring at the girl. "Sumi's dead."

The girl stared at Nadya. The girl bent, reaching into the pond, and came up with a turtle, which she hurled as hard as she could at Nadya's head. Nadya ducked. The girl's dress, finally chewed to pieces by the water, fell off entirely, leaving her naked and covered with a pinkish slime. Cora put her hand over her eyes.

Maybe leaving her room today hadn't been the best idea after all.

• • •

Most people assumed, upon meeting Cora, that being fat also meant she was lazy, or at least that she was unhealthy. It was true she had to wrap her knees and ankles before she did any heavy exercise—a few strips of tape now could save her from a lot of aching later—but that was as far as that assumption went. She had always been a runner. When she'd been little, her mother hadn't worried about her weight, because no one who watched Cora race around the yard could possibly believe there was anything wrong with her. She was chubby because she was preparing for a growth spurt, that was all.

The growth spurt, when it had come, hadn't been enough to consume Cora's reserves, but still she ran. She ran with the sort of speed that people thought should be reserved for girls like Nadya, girls who could cut through the wind like knives, instead of being borne along like living clouds, large and soft and swift.

She reached the front steps with feet pounding and arms pumping, so consumed by the act of running that she wasn't exactly looking where she was going, and slammed straight into Christopher, sending both of them sprawling. She yelped. Christopher shouted. They landed in a tangle of limbs at the base of the porch, him mostly under her.

"Uh," said Christopher.

"Ohfuck!" The exclamation came out as a single word, glued together by stress and terror. This was it: this was the moment where she stopped being the new student, and became the clumsy fat girl. She pushed herself away from him as fast as she could, overbalancing in the process, so that she rolled away rather than getting back to her feet. When she was far enough that they were no longer in physical contact, she shoved herself up onto her hands and knees, looking warily back at him. He was going to yell, and then she was going to cry, and meanwhile Nadya would be alone with the stranger who was asking for a dead person. And this day had started so *well*.

Christopher was staring back at her, looking equally wary, looking equally *wounded*. As she watched, he picked his bone flute out of the dust and said, in a hurt tone, "It's not contagious, you know."

"What's not contagious?"

"Going to a world that wasn't all unicorns and rainbows. It's not catching. Touching me doesn't change where you went."

Cora's cheeks flared red. "Oh, no!" she said, hands fluttering in front of her like captive parrotfish, trying to escape. "I didn't—I wasn't—I mean, I—"

"It's okay." Christopher stood. He was tall and lean, with brown skin and black hair, and a small, skull-shaped pin on his left lapel. He always wore a jacket, partially for the pockets, and partially for the readiness to run. Most of them were like that. They always had their shoes, their scissors, whatever talisman they wanted to have to hand when their doorways reappeared and they had to make the choice to stay or go. "You're not the first."

"I thought you were going to be mad at me for running into you and call me fat," blurted Cora.

Christopher's eyebrows rose. "I . . . okay, not what I expected. I, um. Not sure what to say to that."

"I *know* I'm fat, but it's all in how people say it," said Cora, hands finally drifting back to rest. "I thought you'd say it the bad way."

"I get it," said Christopher. "I'm Mexican-American. It was gross, the number of people at my old school who thought it was funny to call me an anchor baby, or to ask, all fake concerned, if my parents were legal. It got to where I didn't want to say 'Mexican,' because it sounded like an insult in their mouths when it was really my culture, and my heritage, and my family. So I get it. I don't like it, but that's not your fault."

"Oh, good," said Cora, sighing her relief. Then she wrinkled her nose and said, "I have to go. I have to find Miss Eleanor."

"Is that why you were in such a hurry?"

"Uh-huh." She nodded quickly. "There's a strange girl in the turtle pond and she says she's the daughter of someone I've never heard of, but who Nadya says is dead, so I think we need an adult."

"If you need an adult, you should be looking for Kade, not Eleanor," said Christopher. He started toward the door. "Who's the dead person?"

"Someone named Sumi."

Christopher's fingers clamped down hard on his bone flute. "Walk faster," he said, and Cora did, following him up the steps and into the school.

The halls were cool and empty. There were no classes in session; the other students would be scattered across the campus, chatting in the kitchen, sleeping in their rooms. For a place that could explode with noise and life under the right circumstances, it was often surprisingly quiet.

"Sumi was a student before you got here," said Christopher. "She went to a world called Confection, where she pissed off the Countess of Candy Floss and got herself kicked out as a political exile."

"Did her parents take her away?"

"She was murdered."

Cora nodded solemnly. She had heard about the murders, about the girl named Jill who had decided the way to open her own door home was to cut away the doors of as many others as she deemed necessary. There was a certain amount of horror in those tales, and also a certain amount of shameful understanding. Many of them—not all, not even most, but many—would have done the same if they'd had the necessary skills. Some people even seemed to possess a certain grudging respect for what Jill had done. Sure, she'd killed people. In the end, it had been enough to take her home.

"The person who killed her wasn't a friend of mine, not really, but her sister kind of was. We were . . . Jack and Jill went to a world called the Moors, which was sort of horror movie-y, from the way they described it. A lot of people lumped me in with them, because of Mariposa."

"That's the world you went to?"

Christopher nodded. "Eleanor still can't decide whether it was a Fairyland or an Underworld or something new and in-between. That's why people shouldn't get too hung up on labels. Sometimes I think that's part of what we do wrong. We try to make things make sense, even when they're never going to."

Cora didn't say anything.

The hall ended at the closed door to Eleanor's studio. Christopher rapped his knuckles twice against the wood, then opened it without waiting to be asked.

Eleanor was inside, a paintbrush in her hand, layering oil paint onto a canvas that looked like it had already been subjected to more than a few layers. Kade was there as well, sitting in the window seat, a coffee mug cupped between his hands. Both of them looked at the open door, Eleanor with delight, Kade with slow confusion.

"Cora!" she said. "Have you come to paint with me, dear? And Christopher. It's wonderful to see you making friends, after everything."

Christopher grimaced. "Yes, Miss Eleanor," he said. "We're not actually here for an art class. There's someone in the turtle pond."

"Is it Nadya?" asked Kade.

"Not this time," said Cora. "She fell out of the sky, and she has black hair, and her dress fell apart when it got wet, and she says—" She stopped, reaching a degree of impossibility past which even she, who had once fought the Serpent of Frozen Tears, could not proceed.

Luckily, Christopher had no such boundaries. "She says Sumi's her mother. Can someone please come to the turtle pond and figure out what the hell is going on?"

Kade sat up straight. "I'll go," he said.

"Go," said Eleanor. "I'll clean up here. Bring her to the office when you're finished."

Kade nodded and slid off his seat, leaving his mug behind as he hurried to collect Cora and Christopher and usher them both out the door. Eleanor watched the three of them go, silent. When the door was closed behind them, she put her head down in her hands.

Sumi's world, Confection, had been a

33

Nonsense world, untethered to the normal laws that governed the order of things. There had been a prophecy of some sort, saying that Sumi would one day return, and overthrow the armies of the Queen of Cakes, establishing her own benevolent monarchy in its place. It wasn't unreasonable to think that the future had felt comfortable going about its business, once there was a prophecy. And now Sumi was dead, and the future, whatever it had once been, was falling apart.

Everything did, if left long enough to its own devices. Futures, pasts, it didn't matter. Everything fell apart.

3 DEAD WOMAN'S DAUGHTER

The stranger was no longer in the turtle pond. That was an improvement, of a sort, but only of a sort: without the water and the turtles to drape her, the stranger had no clothes remaining at all. She was standing naked in the mud, arms crossed, glowering at Nadya, who was trying to look at anything but her.

Christopher whistled as he came over the rise, walking to the left of Kade. Cora, who was on Kade's right, blushed red and turned her eyes away.

"She looks sort of like Sumi, if Sumi were older, and taller, and hotter," said Christopher. "Did someone place an order with a company that drops beautiful Japanese girls from the sky? Do they take special requests?"

"The only kind of girl you'd want dropped on you comes from a medical supply company," said Kade.

Christopher laughed. Cora blushed even harder.

Nadya, who had spotted the three of them, was waving her arms frantically over her head, signaling her distress. In case this wasn't enough, she shouted, "Over here! Next to the naked lady!"

"A cake's a cake, whether or not it's been frosted," said the stranger primly.

"You are not a cake, you are a *human being,* and I can see your *vagina,*" snapped Nadya.

The stranger shrugged. "It's a nice one. I'm not ashamed of it."

Kade walked a little faster.

Once he was close enough to speak without needing to shout, he said, "Hello. I'm Kade West. I'm the assistant headmaster here at Eleanor West's Home for Wayward Children. Can I help you?"

The naked girl swung around to face him, dropping her arms and beginning to gesticulate wildly. The fact that she was now talking to two boys, in addition to the two girls who had been there when she fell out of the sky, didn't appear to trouble her at all.

"I'm looking for my *mother,*" she said loudly. "She was here, and now she's not, and I have a problem, so find her and give her back *right now,* because I need her more than you do!"

"Slow down," said Kade, and because he made the request sound so reasonable, the stranger stopped shouting and simply looked at him, blinking wide and slightly bewildered eyes. "Let's start with something easy. What's your name?"

"Onishi Rini," said the stranger—said Rini. She

really did look remarkably like Sumi, if Sumi had been allowed to live long enough to finish working her way through the kinks and dead-end alleys of puberty, growing tall and lithe and high-breasted. Only her eyes were different. They were a shocking shade of orange, for the most part, with a thin ring of white around the pupils and a thin ring of yellow around the outside of the irises.

She had candy corn eyes. Kade looked at them and knew, without question, without doubt, that she was Sumi's daughter, that in some future, some impossible, broken future, Sumi had been able to make it home to her candy corn farmer. That somewhere, somehow, Sumi had been happy, until somehow her past self had been murdered, and everything had come tumbling down.

Sometimes living on the outskirts of Nonsense simply wasn't fair.

"I'm Kade," he said. "These are my friends, Christopher, Cora, and Nadya."

"I'm not his friend," said Nadya. "I'm a Drowned Girl." She bared her teeth in mock-threat.

Kade ignored her. "It's nice to meet you, Rini. I just wish it were under slightly better circumstances. Will you come back to the house with me? I manage the school wardrobe. I can find you something to wear."

"Why?" asked Rini peevishly. "Are you

37

insulted by my vagina too? Do people in this world not have them?"

"Many people do, and there's nothing wrong with them, and also that's your vulva, but it's considered a little rude to run around showing your genitals to people who haven't asked," said Kade. "Eleanor is in the house, and once you're dressed, we can sit down and talk."

"I don't have time to talk," said Rini. "I need my mother. Please, where is she?"

"Rini—"

"You don't *understand!*" Rini's voice was an anguished howl. She held out her left hand. "I don't have time!"

"Huh," said Nadya.

That was the only thing any of them said. The rest were busy looking at Rini's left hand, with its two missing fingers. They hadn't been cut off: there was no scar tissue. She hadn't been born that way: the place where her fingers should have been was too obviously empty, like a hole in the world. They were simply gone, fading from existence as her own future caught up to the idea that somehow, someway, her mother had never been able to conceive her, and so she had never been born.

Rini lowered her hand. "Please," she repeated.

"This changes things," said Kade. "Come on."

Rini was tall and thin, but many of the students were tall and thin: too many, as far as Cora was concerned. She didn't like the idea that people who already had socially acceptable bodies would get the adventures, too. She knew it was a small and petty thought, one she shouldn't have had in the first place, much less indulged, but she couldn't stop herself from feeling how she felt. Rini had the fashion sense of a drunken mockingbird, attracted to the brightly colored and the shiny, and that, too, was not uncommon among the students, many of whom had traveled to worlds where the idea of subtlety was ignored in favor of the much more entertaining idea of hurting people's eyes.

In the end, Kade had coaxed her into a rainbow sundress, dyed so that the colors melded into each other like a scoop of sherbet in the sun. He had given her slippers for her feet, both in the same style and size, but dyed differently, so that one was poppy orange and the other turquoise blue. He had given her ribbons to tie in her hair, and now they were sitting, the five of them, in Eleanor's parlor.

Eleanor sat behind her desk, hands laced tight together, like a child about to undertake her evening prayers.

"—and that's why she can't be dead," concluded Rini. Her story had been long and rambling and at times nonsensical, full of political coups and popcorn-ball fights, which were like snowball fights, only stickier. She looked around at the rest of them, expression somewhere between triumphant and hopeful. She had made her case, laid it out in front of them one piece at a time, and she was ready for her reward. "So please, can we go and tell her to stop? I need to exist. It's important."

"I'm so sorry, dear, but death doesn't work that way in this world," said Eleanor. Each word seemed to pain her, driving her shoulders deeper and deeper into their slump. "This is a logical world. Actions have consequences here. Dead is dead, and buried is buried."

Rini frowned. "That's silly and it's stupid and *I'm* not from a logical world, and neither is my mother, so that shouldn't matter for us. I need her back. I need to be born. It's important. *I'm* important."

"Everyone is important," said Eleanor.

Rini looked around at the rest of them. "Please," she pleaded. "Please, make the silly old woman stop being awful, and give me back my mother."

"Don't call my aunt a silly old woman," said Kade.

"It's all right, dear," said Eleanor. "I *am* a silly old woman, and I've been called worse with less reason. I can't fix this. I wish I could."

Cora, who had been frowning more and more since Rini had finished her story, looked up, looked at Rini, and asked, "How did you get here?"

"I just told you," said Rini. "My mother and father had sex before bringing in the candy corn harvest, the year after she defeated the Queen of Cakes at the Raspberry Bridge. You do have sex here, don't you? Or do people in a logical world reproduce by budding? Is that why you were so upset by my vagina?"

Kade put his hand over his face.

"Um," said Cora, cheeks flaring red. "Yes, we, uh, we have sex, and can we please stop saying 'vagina' so much, but I meant how did you get *here*. How did you wind up in our turtle pond?"

"Oh!" Rini held up her right hand, the one that still had all its fingers and had yet to start fading from existence. There was a bracelet clasped around her wrist, the sort of thing a child might wear, beads on a piece of string tied tight to keep her from losing it. "The Fondant Wizard gave me a way for back-and-forth, so I could get here and find Mom and tell her to stop doing whatever she was doing that was making me never have been born. I'm supposed to be sneaking through the Treacle Bogs right now, you know, to look for threats along our western border. Important stuff. So if we could hurry up, that would be amazing."

Silence followed her words, silence like a bowstring, stretched tight and ready to snap. Slowly, Rini lowered her arm and looked around. Everyone was staring at her. Christopher was swallowing hard, the muscles in his throat

41

jumping wildly. There were tears in Nadya's eyes.

"What?" she asked.

"Why did you leave her here?" Kade's voice was suddenly low and dangerous. He stood, stalking toward Rini. "When Sumi got to the school, she was a *mess*. I thought we were gonna lose her. I thought she was going to slice herself open to try to get the candy out of her veins, and now here you are, and you have something that means you can just . . . just come here and go back again, like it's nothing. Like the doors don't even matter. Why did you leave her here? Why didn't someone come and get her before it was too late?"

Rini shied back, away from him, glancing frantically to Christopher and Nadya for support. Nadya looked away. Christopher shook his head.

"I didn't know!" she cried. "Mom always said she'd loved it here at your school, that she made friends and learned stuff and got her head straight enough to know that she wanted it to be crooked! She never asked me to come get her sooner!"

"If she had, you might never have been born," said Eleanor. She cleared her throat before saying, a little more loudly, "Dearest, please don't torture our guest. Done is done and past is past, and while we're looking for a way to change that, I think we should focus on what can still be done, and what hasn't already been omitted."

"Can those beads take us anywhere?" asked Christopher. "Any world at all?"

"Sure," said Rini. "Anywhere there's sugar."

His fingers played across the surface of his bone flute, coaxing out the ghosts of notes. No one could hear them, but that didn't matter. He knew that they were there.

"I think I know a way to fix this," he said.

The basement room that had belonged to Jack and Jill, before they returned to the Moors, and to Nancy, before she returned to the Halls of the Dead, belonged to Christopher now. He viewed it with a certain superstitious hope, like the fact that its last three occupants had been able to find their doors meant that he would absolutely find his own. Magical thinking might seem like nonsense to some people, but he had danced with skeletons by the light of a marigold moon, he had kissed the glimmering skull of a girl with no lips and loved her as he had never loved anything or anyone in his life, and he thought he'd earned a certain amount of nonsense, as long as it helped him get by.

He led the others across the room to the velvet curtain that hung across a rack of metal shelves.

"Jack didn't take anything with her when she left," he said. "I mean, nothing except Jill. Her arms were sort of full." Jack had carried Jill over the threshold like a bride on her wedding night, walking back into the unending wasteland that was their shared perfection, and she hadn't looked back, not once. Sometimes Christopher still dreamt that he had followed her, running away to a world that would never have made him happy, but which might have made him slightly less miserable than this one.

"So?" asked Nadya. "Jack and Jill were creepy fish."

"So I have all her things, and all *Jill's* things, and Jill was building the perfect girl." He pulled the curtain aside, revealing a dozen jars filled with amber liquid and . . . other things. Parts of people that had no business being viewed in isolation.

Christopher leaned up onto his toes, taking a gallon jar down from one of the higher shelves. A pair of hands floated inside, preserved like pale starfish, fingers spread in eternal surprise.

Kade's voice was frosty. "We buried those," he said.

"I know," said Christopher. "But I started having bad dreams after Sumi's family took her away to bury her. Dreams about her skeleton being incomplete forever. So I . . . well, I got a shovel, and I got her hands. I dug up her hands. That way, if she ever came back, I could put her together again. She wouldn't have to be broken forever."

Kade stared at him. "Christopher, are you

honestly telling me you've been sharing a bedroom with Sumi's *severed hands* this whole time? Because boy, that ain't normal." His Oklahoma accent, always stronger when he was upset, was thick as honey.

Rini, on the other hand, didn't appear disturbed in the slightest. She was looking at the jar with wide, interested eyes. "Those are my mother's hands?" she asked.

"Yes," said Christopher. He held the jar carefully as he turned to the others. "If we know where Sumi is buried, I can put her back together. I mean, I can pipe her out of the grave and give her back her hands."

"What?" asked Cora.

"Ew," said Nadya.

"Skeletons don't usually have children," said Kade. "What are you suggestin'?"

Christopher took a deep breath. "I'm suggesting we get Sumi out of the grave, and then we go and find Nancy. She's in the Halls of the Dead, right? She's got to know where the ghosts go. Maybe she can tell us where Sumi went, and we can . . . put her back together."

Silence fell again, speculative this time. Finally, Eleanor smiled.

"That makes no sense at all," she said. "That means it may well work. Go, my darlings, and bring your lost and shattered sister home."

PART II
INTO THE HALLS OF THE DEAD

4 WHAT WE BURY IS NOT LOST, ONLY SET ASIDE

Of the five of them who were going on this journey—Nadya and Cora, Rini, Christopher and Kade—only Kade knew how to drive, and so he was the one stuck behind the wheel of the school minivan, eyes on the road and prayers on his lips as he tried to focus on getting them where they were going in one piece.

Rini had never been in a car before, and kept unfastening her seatbelt because she didn't like the way it pinched. Nadya claimed she could only ride with all the windows down, while Cora didn't like being cold, and kept turning the heat up. Christopher, meanwhile, insisted on turning the volume on the radio up as far as it would go, which didn't make a damn bit of sense, since usually the songs he played were inaudible to anyone who wasn't dead.

It was going to be a miracle if they got where they were going without getting themselves killed. Kade supposed that joining Sumi in whatever afterlife she was in—presumably one that catered to teenagers who'd gone through impossible doors—would be a bad thing. All of them winding up dead would upset Eleanor, as well as leaving the school without a van. Kade ground his teeth and focused on the road.

This would have been easier if they'd been driving during the day. Sumi's remaining family lived six hours from the school grounds, and her body was interred at a local cemetery. That was good. Grave robbing was still viewed as socially inappropriate, and doing it when the sun was up was generally viewed as unwise. Which meant it was after midnight and they were on the road, and everything about this little adventure was a terrible idea from start to finish.

Nadya leaned over the seat to ask, "Are we there yet?"

"Why are you even here?" Kade countered. "You can't pipe the dead out of the ground, you can't drive, and we'd be a lot more comfortable with only three people in the backseat."

"I got doused in turtle water," said Nadya. "That means I get to come."

Kade sighed. "I want to argue, but I'm too damn tired. Can you at least stay in your seat? We get pulled over, we're going to have one hell of a time explaining the severed hands, or why Christopher keeps a human ulna in his pocket."

"Just tell them we're on a quest," said Nadya.

"Mmm," said Kade noncommittally.

"So are we there yet?"

"Almost. We are almost there." The cemetery

was another five miles down the road. He'd looked it up on Google Maps. There was a convenient copse of trees about a quarter of a mile away. They could stow the van there while they went about the business of desecrating Sumi's grave.

Kade wasn't religious—hadn't been since he'd come back from Prism, forced into a body that was too young and too small and too dressed in frilly, girlish clothes by parents who refused to understand that they had a son and not a daughter—but he'd been to church often enough when he was little to be faintly worried that they were all going to wind up getting smote for crimes against God.

"Not the way I wanted to die," he muttered, and pulled off the road, driving toward the trees.

"I want to die in a bed of marigolds, with butterflies hanging over me in a living canopy and the Skeleton Girl holding our marriage knife in her hand," said Christopher.

"What?" said Kade.

"Nothing," said Christopher.

Kade rolled slowly to a stop under a spreading oak, hopefully out of sight of the road, and parked. "All right, we're here. Everybody out."

He didn't have to tell Cora twice. She had the door open before he had finished speaking, practically tumbling out into the grass. Riding in backseats always made her feel huge and

51

worthless, taking up more space than she had any right to. The only reason she'd been able to stand it was that Nadya had been crammed into the middle, leaving Rini, still a virtual stranger, on the other side of the car. If Cora had been told she'd have to spend the entire drive pressed against someone she didn't know, she would probably have skipped having an adventure in favor of hiding in her room.

The others got out more sedately, even Rini, who turned in a slow circle, eyes turned toward the sky and jaw gone slack.

"What are those?" she asked, jabbing a finger at the distant streak of the Milky Way.

"Stars, stupid," said Nadya.

"I'm not stupid, I just don't know stuff," said Rini. "How do they stay up?"

"They're very far away," said Kade. "Don't you have stars in Confection?"

"No," said Rini. "There's a moon—it's made of buttercream frosting, very sticky, not good for picnicking on—and there's a sun, and a long time ago, the First Confectioner threw handfuls of candy into the sky, where it stuck really high, but it's still candy. You can see the stripes on the humbugs and the sugar speckles on the gumdrops."

"Huh," said Kade. He looked to Christopher. "We need a shovel?"

"Not if she's willing to dance." Christopher's fingers played over his bone flute, sketching anxious arpeggios, outlining the tune he would play for Sumi. "If she's willing to dance, she'd move heaven and earth to come to me."

"Then lead the way, piper."

Christopher nodded and raised his flute to his mouth, taking a deep breath before he began to play. There was no sound. There was never any sound when Christopher played the flute, not as far as the living were concerned. There was only the idea of sound, the sketchy outline of the place where it should have been, sliced out of the air like a piece of chocolate pie.

No one knew how far he could be from the dead and still call them out of the grave, and they weren't sure exactly where in the cemetery Sumi's body was buried, and so he played as they walked toward the gates, putting everything he had into calling her and only her, Sumi, the wild girl who died too soon and too cruelly, rather than all the sleeping bones the graveyard had to offer. It had been too long since he'd been to a proper dance, one where the women wore garlands of flowers low on their hips and the men rattled their finger bones like castanets, where the dancers traded garments and genders and positions as easily as trading a blossom for a bolero. It was tempting, to call all the skeletons of this place to him, to lose himself in a revel while the moon was high.

But that wouldn't save Rini, and it wouldn't be

what he had promised Miss Eleanor he'd do. So he played for an audience of one, and when he heard Cora gasp, he smiled around his flute and continued fingering the stops, calling Sumi from her slumber.

She came, a lithe, delicate skeleton wrapped in a pearlescent sheen, like opal, like sugar glass. The cemetery gates had been designed to keep the living out, not the dead in; she stepped sideways and slipped right through the bars, her fleshless body fitting perfectly in the gap. Christopher stopped walking but kept playing as Sumi, risen from the grave, walked across the field to meet them.

"Where's the *rest* of her?" demanded Nadya.

"He doesn't pipe flesh, only bone," said Kade. "He's called what will listen to him." The flesh, softened by time, if not yet rotted away, must have shrugged away like an old overcoat, leaving Sumi shining, wrapped in rainbows, to answer Christopher's call.

Rini raised her hands to cover her mouth. Another of her fingers was gone, replaced by that strange, eye-rejecting void. "Mom?" she whispered.

Sumi cocked her head to the side, more like a bird than a girl, and said nothing. Christopher hesitated before lowering his flute. When Sumi didn't collapse into a pile of bones, he let out a long sigh, shoulders slumping with relief.

"She can't talk," he said. "She doesn't have lungs, or a voice, or anything." At home in Mariposa, she would have been able to speak. The magic that powered that land was happy to give a voice to the dead.

But this was not his home. Here, skeletons were silent, and only the sliver of Mariposa that he carried always with him was even enough to call them from the grave.

"She's dead," said Rini, like she was realizing this for the first time. "How can she be dead?"

"Everyone is, eventually," said Christopher. "This next part is harder. Cora, can you open the jar with her hands, please?"

Cora grimaced as she knelt and wrested the lid off the jar, spilling sharp-smelling liquid onto the ground. She looked to Christopher. On his nod, she dumped the jar's contents out, jumping to her feet and stumbling back to avoid the splash.

Christopher raised his flute and began to play again.

"I'm going to barf," announced Nadya.

The flesh on Sumi's hands began peeling back like a flower in the process of opening, revealing clean white bone. As they all watched, the bone grew bright with rainbows, like the rest of Sumi's skeleton.

When the flesh had peeled away entirely, Christopher tucked his flute into his belt and bent to pick up the two skeletal hands. He offered them to Sumi. She leaned forward and touched the severed ends of her wrists to the base of the carpals. The rainbow glow intensified. She leaned back again, and she was whole, every bone in its place, every piece of her skeleton where it belonged.

"If we're trying to get to an Underworld, starting from a cemetery seems like the best way to do it," said Christopher. He looked to Rini. "You can tell those beads where to take us, right?"

"I can tell them who I want, and they get me there," said Rini. "I couldn't find my mother, no matter how hard I looked, so I looked for Miss Elly. That was who Mom always said made the school go."

"Okay," said Christopher. "Tell the bead to take us to Nancy."

"I don't know Nancy," protested Rini.

"Nancy's smart," said Kade. "She's quiet, so sometimes people don't know she's smart, but the smart's always there."

"She can stand so still she looks like a statue," said Christopher.

"She has white hair with black streaks in it and she says it isn't dyed and her roots never grew out so she probably wasn't lying," said Nadya. The others looked at her, and she shrugged. "We weren't *friends*. I had one group therapy session with her, and stayed out of her way. Too dry for me. Dry as bones."

Cora, who had come to the school after Nancy was already gone, said nothing at all.

Rini frowned at each of them in turn. "What about the sugar?"

"Red," said Kade. "They mix it with pomegranate juice. It's bitter, but it still sweetens." His gaze remained steady, fixed on her. The fact that he had never seen the sugar in Nancy's world didn't matter. He knew what it *should* be, and that was as good as knowing what it *was*.

Rini nodded before lifting her wrist to her mouth and taking one of the beads on her bracelet between her teeth. She bit down hard, the bead shattering with a crunch, and swallowed.

"Wait," said Nadya. "*Those* are sugar, too?"

"Where I come from, everything is sugar," said Rini. She reached imperiously in front of herself, grasping an invisible doorknob. "Come on. They never stay open long, and sometimes they don't match up very well."

"Hence the falling out of the sky, one assumes," said Christopher.

Rini nodded, and opened the door that wasn't there.

The other side was a grove of trees with dark green leaves and gently twisted trunks. Their boughs were heavy with red fruit. Some of it had split open, showing the ruby seeds within. The grass around the trees looked soft as velvet, and the sky was no sky at all, but the high, vaulted ceiling of an impossible hall.

"The pomegranate grove," breathed Kade.

"It's the right place? Good," said Rini. "Come on." She stepped through the door, with the skeleton of her mother close on her heels. The others followed, and when it swung shut behind Cora, it wasn't there anymore, just like it had never been there in the first place.

5 PLACES OF THE LIVING, PLACES OF THE DEAD

The six of them—five living, one dead—walked through the velvety grass, making no attempt to disguise their gawking. Christopher kept his bone flute in his hand, fingers tracing silent arpeggios. Sumi stayed close to her daughter, bones clacking faintly, like the distant whisper of wind through the branches of a tree. Rini tried her best not to look back. Every time she caught a glimpse of Sumi she shuddered and bit her lip before looking away again.

Nadya reached up with her single hand and traced the outline of a pomegranate with her fingers, biting her lip and staring at the fruit like it was the most beautiful thing she had ever seen.

"Nancy said she spent most of her time as a statue in the Lady's hall," said Kade, pushing forward until he was in the lead. No one questioned him. It was good to have *someone* willing to be the leader. "I suppose that means she might be there now."

"Is the Lord of the Dead going to be happy to see us?" asked Nadya, finally taking her hand away from the pomegranate.

"Maybe," said Kade. "He's got doors. He's got to be used to people stumbling in without an invitation."

"But you only find doors you're suited to," said Cora. "We didn't *find* this one. We made it. Won't he be upset about that?"

"Only one way to find out," said Kade, and started walking.

"Why do people always *say* that?" muttered Cora, trailing along at the rear of the group. "There's always more than one way to find something out. People only say there's only one way when they want an excuse to do something incredibly stupid without getting called on it. There are *lots* of ways to find out, and some of them even involve not pissing off a man who goes by 'the *Lord* of the *Dead*.'"

"Yeah, but they wouldn't be as much fun, now would they?"

Cora glanced to the side. Christopher had dropped back to walk beside her. He was grinning, looking more at ease than she had ever seen him.

"Why are you so happy?" she asked. "Everything here is dead people."

"That's why I'm so happy," he said. "Everything here is dead people."

Somehow, when he said it, it wasn't a complaint, or even an observation: it was virtually a prayer, packed with hope and homecoming.

This wasn't his world, wasn't Mariposa, and the only skeleton who danced here was poor Sumi. But it was closer than he had been in a long, long time, and she could see the joy coming back into his body with every step he took.

"Do you really want to be a skeleton?" she blurted.

Christopher shrugged. "Everybody's a skeleton someday. You die, and the soft parts drop away, and what's left behind is all beautiful bone. I just want to go back to a place where I don't have to die to be beautiful."

"But you're not fat!" Cora couldn't keep the horror from her voice. She didn't even try. Growing up fat had meant an endless succession of diets suggested by "helpful" relatives, and even more "helpful" suggestions from her classmates, ones that suggested starvation or learning to vomit on command. She'd managed to dodge an eating disorder through luck, and because the swim team had needed her to stay in good shape: if her school hadn't offered endurance swimming as well as speed, if she'd been expected to slim down to be allowed into the water, she would probably have joined the girls behind the gym, the ones who died slowly on a diet of ice chips, black coffee, and cigarettes.

"It's not about fat or thin," said Christopher. "It's not . . . oh, fuck. You probably think this is about dieting, don't you?" He didn't wait for her to reply before he continued: "It's not. It's really not. Mariposa is a land of skeletons. As long as I have skin, as long as I'm like this, they can make me leave. Once the Skeleton Girl and I marry, once she cuts my humanity away, I can stay forever. That's all I want."

"That's all any of us want," admitted Cora.

"You were a mermaid, weren't you? That's what Nadya said."

"I still am," said Cora. "I just have my scales under my skin for now."

Christopher smiled, a little lopsided. "Funny. That's where I keep my bones."

The pomegranate grove was coming to an end around them, the trees growing less frequent as they approached a high marble wall. There was a door there, tall and imposing, the sort of door that belonged on a cathedral or a palace; the sort of door that said "keep out" far more loudly than it would ever dream of saying "come in." But it was standing open, and when they drew nearer, no one appeared to warn them off. Kade glanced back at the others, shrugged, and kept walking, leaving them no choice but to follow.

And then, with so little warning that Cora thought the people who lived here—who existed here—would be fully within their rights to be angry, they were in the Halls of the Dead. The architecture was exactly what a thousand movies had told her to expect: marble pillars holding up impossible ceilings, white stone walls softened with friezes and with watercolor paintings of flowering meadows. The colors were muted, whites and pastel greens and grayish pines. They somehow managed not to become twee, but to project an air of solemnity and silence instead. The only sounds were their feet tapping against the stone floor, and the clacking of Sumi's bones.

"You were not invited, and none of Our doors have opened, nor closed, in this last day," said a woman from behind them: she was between them and the doorway that might have led them back to the pomegranate grove. Her voice was low and husky, like blackberry brandy given a throat. "Who are you? How are you here?"

Cheeks burning, feeling like a child who'd been caught sneaking to the kitchen for a midnight snack, Cora turned, and beheld the Lady of the Dead.

She was short and curvy, with skin the color of polished cypress and hair that fell down her back in a cascade of inky curls, stopping just below her waist. Her eyes were like pomegranate seeds, deep red and as impossible as Rini's candy corn irises, yet just as undeniably real. Her gown was the same color, some loosely draped Grecian style that complimented every curve she had, and made Cora yearn for a fashion as forgiving.

"Well?" asked the Lady. "Have you all been struck silent by My presence? Or are you thinking of excuses? I suggest you not lie to Me. My husband has little patience for those who offer trespass and insult both in the same hour."

"I'm sorry, ma'am," said Kade, pushing his way forward. The relief from the rest of the group was almost palpable. Let someone else take the blame, if there was blame to take. "I know we came uninvited, but we weren't sure how to ring the bell."

"You taste of Fairyland, little hero," said the Lady of the Dead, wrinkling her nose. "All of you taste of something that isn't meant for here, all but him." She pointed to Christopher. "Mirrors and Fairylands and Lakes. Even the skeleton tastes of Mirror. The taint lingers past death. You have no business ringing Our doorbell."

"We're here to beg a favor, ma'am," said Kade doggedly. "This is Rini."

Rini raised her hand in a small wave. She was down to a single finger and her thumb, and half of her palm had melted away, replaced by that same eye-burning nothingness.

"The skeleton is her mother, Sumi, who died before Rini could be born, and now Rini is, well, disappearing," continued Kade. "One of our old classmates lives here with you. We were hoping she might be able to help us find where Sumi's spirit went after she died, so that we can try to put her back together and keep Rini from disappearing altogether. Er. Ma'am."

The Lady of the Dead's eyes widened fractionally. "You're Nancy's friends," she said.

"Yes, ma'am."

"I'm not," said Nadya. "I'm a Drowned Girl."

"So you are," said the Lady of the Dead. She gave Nadya a thoughtful look. "You went to one of the Drowned Worlds, the underground lakes, the forgotten rivers. Many of them touch on Our borders. They aren't Underworlds, but they're under the rest of the world."

Nadya paled. "You know how to get to Belyyreka?" she asked, voice barely above a whisper.

"I didn't say that," said the Lady. "We have no power over the Drowned Worlds. I wouldn't—couldn't—open a door there if you asked Me. But I know the place. It's beautiful."

"It is," agreed Nadya, and started to cry.

The Lady of the Dead turned back to Kade. "You come uninvited, to trouble a handmaiden who still stings from her time in your company. Why should We grant you an audience with her? Why should We grant you anything at all?"

"Because Nancy told us you were kind," said Christopher. He was staring at her in quiet awe, like he hadn't seen anything so beautiful in years. "She said you never made her feel like she was broken just because she was different. You and your husband, you're the reason she wanted to come back here and stay forever. You made this

65

place home. I can't imagine anyone who'd be that kind to Nancy could be cruel enough not to help us."

"Mariposa, wasn't it, for you?" asked the Lady, looking thoughtful. "So many different doors, and yet here you are, all of you together, trying to accomplish the impossible. I'll let you talk to Nancy."

"Thank you, ma'am," said Kade.

"Don't thank me yet," said the Lady. "There are conditions. Eat nothing; drink nothing. Speak to no one save for Myself, My husband, and Nancy. The living who choose to spend their years in these halls do so because they're looking for quiet, for peace, for solitude. They don't need you reminding them that they were hot and fast once. Do you understand?"

"Yes, ma'am," said Kade. The others nodded, even Rini, who looked more confused than anything else. She was doing an excellent job of holding her tongue. For a Nonsense girl in a world full of rules, that was just this side of a miracle.

"Good," said the Lady. "This way."

She turned then, and walked back into the door to the grove, leaving the rest of them to follow.

The trees were gone. In their place was a long hall, the sort that belonged in a palace or a museum, its walls lined with statues, all of them standing beautifully still in their frost-white draperies. No, not statues—*people*. People of all ages, from children barely old enough to have shed their infant proportions to men and women older than Eleanor, their faces seamed with wrinkles, their limbs thinned out by time and trials. There was a certain vitality around them that betrayed their natures, but apart from that, they might as well have been the carved stone they worked so hard to imitate.

Rini shuddered, stepping a little closer to Kade, like she thought he could protect her. "How can they hold so *still?*" she whispered, voice horrified and awed. "I'd twitch myself into pieces."

"That's why this was never your door," he said. "We don't go where we're not meant to be, even if we sometimes get born in the wrong place."

"There was a boy," said Rini. "When I was small. His parents mined fudge from the northern ridge. He didn't like the smell of chocolate, or the way it melted on his tongue. He wanted to be clean, and to follow rules, and to *understand*. He disappeared the year we all started school, and his parents were sad, but they said he'd found his door, and if he was lucky, he'd never come back, not ever, not once."

Kade nodded. "Exactly. Your mother and I were born in the same world, and it wasn't right for either of us, so we went somewhere else." He didn't ask what sort of lessons would be taught at school in a Nonsense world. His own world had been Logical, and what made perfect sense to Rini wouldn't make any sense at all to him.

The people on their pedestals and set back in niches in the walls said nothing, did nothing to show that they were even aware that anyone was nearby. The Lady kept walking, and the rest of them kept following, until she reached a pair of wide marble doors. Leaning forward, she tapped them ever so gently with the tip of her left forefinger, and stood back as they swung open to reveal a room that was half cathedral and half cavern.

The walls were naked gray stone, unshaped, unworked, sweeping upward to a crystal-studded bell of a natural vault. Lights hung from the ceiling, their bases set between great spikes of purple amethyst and silvery quartz, and the floor was polished marble, creating a strange melding of the natural and the manmade.

At the center of the room, well away from any of the walls, was a freestanding dais. Two thrones rested atop it, and short pedestals surrounded it, three to either side, each holding one of the living statues.

The statue closest to the door was Nancy.

Nancy at peace: Nancy in her element. She stood tall and calm and strong, one arm raised in a graceful arc, her chin canted slightly toward the ceiling, calling attention to the delicate line of

her neck, the organic sculpture of her collarbone. She wore a long white gown, like so many of the other statues, but unlike them, there was a wine-red, pomegranate-red ribbon tied around her neck, casting the rest of her into monochrome relief. Someone had styled her white and black hair, arranging it so that the black streaks left by the Lord of the Dead's fingers were perfectly displayed, like the badge of honor that they were.

Christopher whistled low. "Damn, girl," he said.

Kade said nothing. He only stared.

Both thrones were currently empty. The Lady of the Dead led them toward the dais, stopping when they reached Nancy, who must have been aware of their presence, but who did nothing to betray that knowledge.

"Nancy," said the Lady softly. "Please move for Me. You have company."

Nancy moved like frost melting: slowly at first, almost imperceptibly, and then with more speed, until she finished lowering her arm and chin and turned with something approaching, yet far greater than, human grace. She allowed herself to look at the people clustered around the base of her pedestal, and her eyes widened, ever so slightly.

"Kade," she said. "Christopher . . . Nadya?" She looked at the others without recognition. "What are you all doing here? Is everything all right? Are you . . ." She stopped herself. "No, you're not dead. If you were dead, you wouldn't be here."

"We're not dead," said Kade, and smiled. "It's good to see you, Nancy."

"It's good to see you too." She glanced to the Lady of the Dead, seeking permission. The Lady nodded, and Nancy dropped to her knees, sliding into a graceful kneeling position atop her pedestal. It was a practiced, easy motion; she had done this before. "I'm sorry I didn't say goodbye."

"I don't think most of us would," said Kade. "You happy?"

Nancy's smile was brief but brilliant. Artists would have died for the chance to paint that moment of pure, unfettered bliss. "Always."

"Then all is forgiven." Kade gestured for Rini to step forward. "This is Rini. Sumi's daughter."

"What?" Nancy's expression faded into puzzlement at the mention of her former roommate. "Sumi didn't have children. She was too young. She would have told me."

"She was *supposed* to come back to Confection and save the world and get married and make a baby," said Rini. She held up her arm. Her hand was entirely gone now; her flesh ended at the wrist, and at the tear her disappearance was leaving in reality. "She needs to stop being *dead* and come home and have sex until I exist again!"

"Um," said Nancy, looking nonplussed.

"This is Sumi," said Christopher, gesturing to the shimmering skeleton beside him. "We were hoping you might know where the rest of her is."

"You mean her *ghost?*" asked Nancy.

"Yes," said Christopher.

Sumi said nothing, but she cocked her shining skull to the side in a gesture that was a pale shadow of her constant curious motion before she had died, her skin and flesh stripped away, leaving her in silence.

"Even if . . ." Nancy glanced to the Lady, who nodded permission. "Even if I could find Sumi's ghost for you, even if she was *here,* how would you put her back together? You'd still be missing all the . . . squishy bits."

"Let us worry about that," said Kade.

Nancy looked to the Lady again. Again, the Lady nodded her assent. Nancy looked back to the others.

"Not all ghosts come here," she said. "This isn't the only Underworld. She could be in a thousand places, or she could be nothing at all. Sometimes people don't want to linger, and so they just disappear."

"Can we try?" asked Kade. "It seems like dying when you still had a world to save might be cause enough to stick around for a little while. And you were roommates when she was alive. Sumi never did like to be alone."

"Even if you can find her ghost, that's just the part of her that's waiting to be reborn," said Nancy. "Who she *was* isn't going to be here."

"We have to try," said Rini. "There's nowhere else to go."

Nancy sighed, a deep, slow sound that started at her toes and traveled all the way up her body. She uncurled her legs and slid down from her pedestal, landing without a sound. As she fell, her skirt rode up just enough for Kade to see that her feet were bare, and that there was a ring on every one of her toes, shimmering and silver.

"Follow me," she said, and bowed to the Lady, and walked away. Every step she took chimed like a bell as the rings on her toes struck the ground.

Kade followed her, and the rest followed him, and they left the remaining statues and the Lady of the Dead behind.

Kade stole glances at Nancy as they walked, trying to memorize the new shape of her face. She was thinner, but not alarmingly so; this was the thinness of a professional athlete at the top of their game, the thinness of someone who did something physical every hour of the day. Her hair was still white, her eyes were still dark, and she was still beautiful. God, but she was beautiful.

Nadya shoved her way between them,

demanding, "So is that all you do all day? You *stand* there? You left a whole world full of shit to do and people to talk to so you could *stand* there?"

"It's more than just standing there," said Nancy. "Hello, Nadya. You're looking well."

"I'm drying out, and this world has no good rivers," said Nadya.

"We have a few." Nancy shook her head. "I don't 'just stand there.' It's like a dance, done entirely in stillness. I have to freeze so completely that my heart forgets to beat, my cells forget to age. Some of the statues have been here for centuries, slowing themselves to the point of near-immortality for the sake of gracing our Lord's halls. It's an honor and a calling, and I love it. I love it so much."

"It seems stupid."

"That's because you weren't called," said Nancy, and that was true, and simple, and complete: it needed neither ornamentation nor addition.

Nadya looked away.

Kade took a breath. "Things have been going well at the school," he said. "Aunt Eleanor's feeling better. She hardly uses her cane these days. We have some new students."

"You brought one of them with you," said Nancy. She laughed a little. "Is it weird that I kind of feel like that's more disturbing than you bringing a skeleton?"

"Her name's Cora. She's nice. She was a mermaid."

"Then she still is," said Nancy. "There's always hope."

"Sumi used to say that hope was a four-letter word."

"She was right. That's why it never goes away." They had reached another closed door, this one a filigree of silver, containing an infinity of blackness. Nancy raised her hand. The door swung open and she continued through, into the dark—which was, once entered, not so total after all.

Gleaming silver sparks swirled through the air, darting and flitting around the room, as swift and restless as the rest of the Halls of the Dead were still. They would fly close to a nose or a cheek, only to jerk away at the last second, never quite touching living flesh.

Rini gasped. Everyone turned.

Sumi was covered in the dots of light. They clustered on her bones, hundreds of them, with more arriving every second. She was holding up her skeletal hands like she was admiring them, studying the shimmering specks of light that perched on her phalanges. Dots of light had even filled her eye sockets, replacing her empty gaze with something disturbingly vital.

"If she's here, she's one of these," said Nancy, spreading her arms to indicate the room. "The souls who come to rest here arrive in this room first. They dance their restlessness away before they incarnate again. Call her, and see if she comes."

"Christopher?" said Kade.

"I play for skeletons, not souls," protested Christopher, even as he raised his flute to his mouth and blew a silent, experimental note. The specks of light abandoned Sumi, rising into the air and swirling wildly around him. He continued to play, until, bit by bit, some of the light peeled away and returned to the air, while some of the light began to coalesce in front of Sumi's skeleton. Bit by bit, particle by particle, it came together, until the glowing, translucent ghost of a teenage girl was standing there.

She wore a sensible school uniform, white knee socks, plaid skirt, and buttoned blazer. Her hair was pulled into low braids, tamed, contained. It was Sumi, yes, but Sumi rendered motionless, Sumi stripped of laughter and nonsense. Rini gasped again, this time with pain, and raised her remaining hand and the stump of what had been its twin to cover her mouth.

The specter of Sumi looked at the skeleton. The skeleton looked at the specter.

"Why is she like that?" whispered Rini. "What did you do to my mother?"

"I told you, we have her ghost, but not her shadow—not her heart. Her heart was a wild thing, and this isn't where the wild things go," said Nancy. "If it were, I wouldn't be here. I was never a wild thing." She looked at the shade of Sumi with regret and, yes, love in her eyes. "We're all puzzle boxes, skeleton and skin, soul and shadow. You have two of the pieces now, if she'll go with you, but I don't think her shadow's here."

"Mama . . ." The word belonged to the lips of a much younger girl, meant for bedtimes and bad times, for skinned knees and stomach aches. Rini offered it to Sumi's shade like it was a promise and a prayer at the same time, like it was something precious, to be treasured. "I need you. Please. We need you. The Queen of Cakes will rise again if you don't come home."

The Queen of Cakes would never have been defeated: Sumi had died before she could return to Confection and overthrow the government. Rini wasn't just saving herself. She was saving a world, setting right what was on the verge of going wrong.

The carefully groomed shade of Sumi looked at her blankly, uncomprehending. Nancy, who understood the dead of this place in a way that none of the others did, cleared her throat.

"It will make a mess if you don't go with them," she said.

The shade turned to look at her before nodding and stepping forward, into the skeleton, wreathing the bones in phantom flesh. Rini started to reach for her with her sole remaining hand, and stopped as she saw that two more of her fingers were gone, fading into nothing at all.

"We have to hurry," she said.

"You have to pay," said a new voice.

All of them turned as one. Only Nancy smiled when she saw the man standing in the doorway. He was tall and thin, with skin the color of volcanic ash and hair the color of bone. Like his wife, he wore a flowing garment, almost Grecian in design, which drew the eye to the length of his limbs and the broadness of his shoulders.

"Nothing here is free," he said. "Eat nothing, drink nothing; visitors are told that upon arrival. What makes you think we would give our treasures away, if we will not share our water?" His voice was deep, low, and inevitable, like the death of stars.

"What do you need us to pay, sir?" asked Kade warily.

The Lord of the Dead looked at him with pale and merciless eyes. "One of you will have to stay behind."

6 WE PAY WHAT WE PAY; THE WORLD GOES ON

"No," said Kade, without hesitation. "We're not for sale."

"This isn't a sale," said the Lord of the Dead. "This is an exchange. You want to take one of my residents on a fool's errand. You want to promise her that she can be alive again, when there's no possible way. I would forbid you entirely if I thought you would listen, but you're not the first among the living to seek to play Orpheus and lure what's mine away. Putting a price on the process is the only way to keep you people from robbing me blind."

"Sir," said Nancy, and curtseyed, deep and low. She froze when she was folded fully forward, becoming a statue again.

The Lord of the Dead smiled. He looked strangely human, when he smiled. "My Nancy," he said, and there was no doubting the fondness in his tone. "These are your friends?"

"From school," she said, rising. "This is Kade."

"Ah. The fabled boy." He turned to Kade. "Nancy speaks highly of you."

"Highly enough for you to give us a freebie?"

"Alas."

"Wait." Nadya took a step forward, nervous, glancing around at the others. Her hair, dry after so long away from either bathtub or turtle pond, was a fluffy brown cloud around her head. "Mr. Lord of the Dead, do you have turtles here? Not ghost turtles, I mean. Real turtles, the kind that swim in ponds and do turtle stuff."

"There are turtles in the River of Forgotten Souls," said the Lord of the Dead, looking faintly baffled.

"Okay," said Nadya. "Okay, okay. Because your, um, your wife, she said she knew Belyyreka. That's where my doorway led. To a Drowned World, where I was a Drowned Girl. I still am. It's too dry where I come from. The air doesn't forgive."

"I know the place," said the Lord of the Dead solemnly.

"Doors can open anywhere if the worlds are close enough together, can't they? Rini"—she gestured toward the sniffling girl with the candy corn eyes—"said a boy from the world she comes from found his door and went away, to someplace where he was better suited. If I stayed here, and Belyyreka wanted me back, could my door still find me?"

"Nadya, no," said Cora.

"Yes," said the Lord of the Dead. "And for that, for Belyyreka, I would let you go. For that,

I would stand aside and release all claim to you."

Nadya looked around at the others. "I've been at the school for five years. I'll be seventeen in a month. A year after that and then I graduate, and my family starts expecting me to go somewhere, to make something of my life. I can't live on a countdown. I want to go *home,* and that means waiting until Belyyreka calls me back. I'm not a political exile like Sumi. I'm not a cultural exile like Kade, either. I just got caught in the wrong current. I want to go *home.* I can wait here just as well as I can wait on campus."

"Nadya, *no,*" said Cora, with more desperation. "You can't leave me. You're the only real friend I've got."

Nadya's smile was uneven and quick. "See, that's the best reason for me to stay here. You need to make more friends, Cora. I can't be the only estuary in your waterway."

"Aunt Eleanor's going to kill me," muttered Kade.

"Not when you tell her it was my choice, and that this place is closer to Belyyreka than the school ever was," said Nadya, dismissing his concerns with an airy wave of her hand. She turned to the Lord of the Dead. "If you'll let my friends go, and you'll let me take my door home when it appears, I'll stay with you. I'll haunt your rivers and terrorize your turtles and I'll never be still, but you don't want someone still, or you wouldn't have asked for any of us. You just want someone to stay so you feel like you're in charge of everything."

"Guilty as charged," said the Lord of the Dead, with a very faint smile. "You will stay?"

"I'll stay," said Nadya.

Kade closed his eyes, looking pained.

"The compact is sealed." The Lord of the Dead turned to the group. "Your payment is given; the shade may go with you. Nancy?"

"Yes, milord?"

"Show your friend to the river."

"Yes, milord," said Nancy, and turned to Nadya. "Follow me."

The others stood, silently watching, as the girl who had left them to grace her master's hall led Nadya the Drowned Girl away, toward the river, toward the future, whatever that future might entail. Neither of them looked back. Neither of them said goodbye. The shade-shrouded skeleton of Sumi was a patient reminder of why they had decided to meet this price, and of what it would have to redeem.

"Thank you, sir," said Kade finally. "We'll be going now."

"Wait," said Christopher.

The Lord of the Dead turned to him. "Yes, child of Mariposa?"

"I can pipe the bones of the dead out of the earth, and back in Mariposa, that's enough:

nothing's missing. Something's missing with Sumi. The nonsense didn't come here, Nancy said. Where did it go?"

"The same place nonsense always goes," said the Lord of the Dead. "It went home. Even when a door never opens during the lifetime of a wanderer, they find their rest after death."

"Home . . ." said Kade slowly. He turned to Rini. "All right. Take us to Confection."

Rini's eyes lit up. She didn't hesitate, just raised her bracelet to her mouth and bit off another bead, crunching loudly as she swallowed.

The door opened directly under their feet, swinging wide, and then they were falling, four living teenagers and one glimmering skeleton. Rini laughed all the way down. The door slammed shut behind them.

The Lord of the Dead looked at the place where it had been and sighed before waving his hand, sending the specks of light dancing around the room. The living were always in such a hurry. They would learn soon enough.

Rini's door had opened above what Cora would have called an ocean, had it not been bright pink and gently bubbling. Christopher curled into a ball as he fell, using his entire body to protect his flute. Kade fell like an amateur, all flailing limbs and panic. Rini was laughing, spinning wildly in the air, like she didn't really believe that gravity would hurt her. Sumi's skeleton merely dropped. Dead people probably didn't worry too much about drowning.

Cora, once the surprise powerhouse of her school swim team, curved her body into a bow, arms stretched out in front of her, hands together, head tucked down to reduce the chances of her neck snapping on impact. That didn't happen often. She didn't often see divers leap from this height.

I'm flying, she thought giddily, and who cared if the sea below her was pink and the air around her smelled of sugar and strawberry syrup? Who *cared?* The school had a turtle pond and bathtubs big enough for her to sink down to her nose, only the small islands of her knees and the peak of her belly standing above the surface, but there was no pool, there was no ocean. She hadn't been swimming since she'd left the Trenches, and every molecule of her body yearned for the moment when she would be surrounded by the sea.

They hit the surface all at the same time, Kade and Christopher with enormous splashes, Rini and Sumi with smaller ones, and Cora slicing through the surface of the waves like a harpoon, cutting down, down, down into the pink, bubbling depths.

She was the first to burst back into the air, the force of her mermaid-trained kicks driving her several feet above the pinkish foam as she sputtered and exclaimed, "It's *soda!*"

Rini laughed as she came bobbing back up. "Strawberry rhubarb soda!" she cheered. One of her ears was gone, following her fingers into nothingness. She didn't appear to have noticed. "We're home, we're home, we're home in the foam!" She splashed Cora with her remaining hand, sending soda droplets in all directions.

Kade was sputtering when he surfaced. Sumi's bones simply floated to the top, buoyant beyond all human measure.

Cora frowned. "Where's Christopher?" she asked, looking at Kade.

"What do you mean?"

"I saw where everyone was when we were falling." She had been the only one composed enough to check. The others had been panicking, or plummeting, not trying to get their bearings. She couldn't blame them. Everyone's lives prepared them for something different. "He was right next to you."

Kade's eyes widened. "I don't know."

There wasn't time to keep talking: not if she wanted this to end well. Cora took a deep breath before she dove, wishing briefly that she had a hair tie, or better yet, that she had her gills.

The sea of strawberry rhubarb soda—and who *did* that? They were all going to get horrible urinary tract infections after this—

was translucent, lighter than normal water. The bubbles stung her eyes, but she could deal with the pain. Chlorine was worse.

(It was hard not to think about the damage that sugar and carbonation might do—but Rini wasn't worried, and this was Rini's ocean, in Rini's Nonsense world. Maybe things worked differently here. Things seemed to work differently everywhere she went. Anyway, things had to be at least *slightly* different, or they wouldn't have been able to stay afloat.)

A long eel swam by, seemingly made of living saltwater taffy. The strange shape of its body called to mind the concept of peppermint sharks and turtles with jawbreaker shells, of fish like gumdrops and jellybeans, a whole ecosystem made of living sugar, thriving in a place where the rules were different, where the rules had no concern for how things worked elsewhere. Elsewhere was a legend and a lie, until it came looking for you.

Down, down, down into the strawberry rhubarb sea Cora dove, until she saw something falling slowly through the sea. It looked too solid to be made of candy, and too dark to be prepared for a children's goodie bag. She swam harder, instinctively pressing her legs together and dolphin-kicking her way downward. Even in the absence of fin and scale, she had been the hero of the Trenches, the mermaid who swam as though the Devil himself were behind her. Quickly, she was at Christopher's side, gathering him out of the soda.

His eyes were closed. No bubbles trickled from his nose or mouth. But he was holding his bone flute tightly in one hand. Cora hoped that meant he was still alive. Wouldn't he have let go, if he were already gone?

He wasn't going to let go of the flute. Normally, she would have hooked her hands under his arms, using his armpits to drag him with her, but if that caused him to lose his grip, he was going to insist on going back down to try to find his last piece of home. She could understand that. So she held him to her chest in a parody of a bridal carry, or of the Creature from the Black Lagoon carrying his beautiful victim out of the water. Christopher didn't stir.

Cora kicked.

Sometimes she thought she had always been a mermaid: that her time among the two-legged people had been the fluke, and that her reality was her, well, flukes. She was meant to live a wet and watery existence, free from the tyranny of gravity—which had been trying to ruin her day even more than usual, starting with Rini's fall into the turtle pond. She kicked, and the sea responded, propelling her ever upward, turning effort into momentum.

This, right here, this was what life was supposed

to be. Just her, and an environment where her size was an asset, not an impediment. Her lungs were large. Her legs were strong. She was flying, and even having Christopher clutched in her arms did nothing to slow her down.

They broke the surface of the sea in a spray of soda and bubbles. Rini and Kade were still bobbing there, waiting, as was Sumi's skeleton, which floated like a bath toy for the world's most morbid child.

Christopher's head lolled, his mouth hanging slackly open, a trickle of pink soda running from lips to chin. Cora cast wildly around until she spotted the distant streak of the shore. It wasn't so far: maybe fifty yards. She could do that.

"Come on!" she shouted, and swam, rapidly outpacing her companions. That didn't matter. *They* didn't matter. Christopher was the one who was drowning, who had already drowned. Christopher was the one she had to save.

In what felt like the blink of an eye, she was staggering back onto her unwanted legs, carrying Christopher out of the fizzing waves and onto the shore. It was made of brown sugar and cake crumbs, she realized, as she was in the act of throwing him down onto it. Still he didn't move. She rolled him onto his side, pounding on his back until a gush of pink liquid burst from his mouth, sinking rapidly into the sugary shore. Still he didn't move.

Cora grimaced, realizing what she had to do,

and rolled him onto his back, beginning to go through the steps of CPR. She had taken all the lifeguard courses between ninth and tenth grade, intending to spend the summer sitting by the pool, keeping kids from drowning. Maybe even protecting the shyer, fatter ones from their peers, who would always find reason to make fun.

(She hadn't been counting on her own peers, who had been even more inclined to make fun than their younger brothers and sisters. She hadn't counted on the notes stuffed into her locker, crueler and colder than the ones she received at school, where at least the other students were used to her, had had the time to learn to think of her as something other than "the fat girl." She had never put on her red swimsuit or her whistle. She had done . . . something else, instead, and when she had woken up to find herself in the Trenches, she had thought the afterlife was surprisingly kind, not realizing that this was still the duringlife, and that life would always find a new way to be cruel.)

She breathed for him. She pushed against his chest until finally, it began moving on its own; until Christopher rolled onto his side again, this time under his own power, and vomited a second gush of fizzing pink liquid onto the sand. He began to cough, and she leaned forward, helping him into a sitting position, rubbing slow, soothing circles on his back.

"Breathe," she said. "You need to breathe."

There was a commotion behind her. She didn't turn. She knew what she would see: two people who didn't swim enough staggering out of the waves, with a skeleton following close behind. When that had become the new normal, she couldn't possibly have said.

Christopher coughed again before his head snapped up, eyes widening in alarm. Cora sighed.

"It's in your hand," she said. "You didn't drop it. I wouldn't let you."

He looked down, relaxing slightly when he saw the flute. He still didn't speak.

Cora sat back on her calves, knees folded beneath her, sticky pink liquid soaking every inch of her, and for the first time since leaving the Trenches, she felt almost content. She felt almost like she was home. Turning, she told Kade and Rini, "He's going to be all right."

"Thank God," said Kade. "Aunt Eleanor will forgive me for Nadya deciding to stay behind in an Underworld that might border on her own, but she wouldn't forgive me for a drowning."

"Why wouldn't he have been all right?" asked Rini. "It's just sugar."

"People who don't come from here can die if they breathe too much liquid," said Cora. "It's called 'drowning.'"

Rini looked alarmed. "What a dreadful world you have. I wouldn't want to live in a place where mothers die and people can't breathe the sea."

"Yeah, well, you work with what you have," muttered Cora, thinking about pills and pools and drownings. She turned back to Christopher. "Feel like you can get up?"

He nodded, still silently. Leaning forward, Cora hooked her hands under his arms and stood, pulling him along with her, providing the leverage he needed to get his feet back under himself. Christopher coughed one more time, pressing a hand to the base of his throat.

"Burns," he rasped.

"That's the carbonation," said Cora. "Don't breathe soda. Don't breathe water either, unless you're built for it. Chlorine fucks you up pretty bad too. It'll pass."

Christopher nodded, lowering his hand and letting it join its partner in gripping the bone flute, which was already dry and didn't appear to have been stained by its passage through an infinity of pink dye.

The same couldn't be said for the rest of them. Kade's formerly white shirt was now a pleasant shade of pink, and Rini's dress was less "melting sherbet" and more "strawberry smoothie." Cora had been wearing dark colors, but her white socks weren't anymore. Even Sumi glittered with tiny beads of pink liquid, like jewels in the sun.

"This just keeps getting weirder and I'm not sure I like it," muttered Cora.

Kade gave her a sympathetic look before running a hand back over his hair, releasing a sticky wave of soda. "Try not to think about it too hard. We don't know how much logic this place can handle, and if it starts trying to break us because we're applying too many rules, we're going to have a problem." He turned to Rini. "We're on your home turf now. Where do we go to find your mother's nonsense? We're going to need that if we want to put her back together."

Cora swallowed a cascade of giggles. They would have sounded hysterical, she knew: they would have sounded like she could no longer cope. And that wouldn't have been entirely wrong. She was a solid, practical person, and while she had accepted the existence of magic— sort of hard not to, under the circumstances— there was a lot of ground between "magic is real, other worlds are real, mermaids can be real, in a world that wants them" and "everything is real, women fall out of the sky into turtle ponds, skeletons walk, and we left my best friend in the underworld."

When she got back to the school, she was going to draw herself a hot bath, curl up in the tub, and sleep for *days*.

"This is the Strawberry Sea," said Rini uncomfortably, looking around. "The Meringue Mountains are to the west, and the Big Rock Candy Mountain is to the east. If we chart a course between them, through the Fondant Forests, we should come to the farmlands. That's where my home is. There's where my mother's supposed to be. If her nonsense were going to go anywhere, it would probably go there."

"Just *how* Nonsense is this world, Rini?" asked Kade. "None of us went to nonsensical places, and Nonsense, it tends to reject what doesn't belong inside of it. We tend to haul logic in our wake, like dirt on our shoes."

"I don't understand," said Rini.

"If people don't normally drown when they breathe water here, and Christopher almost drowned, that's logic seeping in," said Kade. "We need to fix your mother and get out of here before the world decides to shove us out."

"Where would we go?" asked Cora.

"That's the sort of philosophical question that my aunt loves and I hate," said Kade. "Maybe we'd go back to the school, or back to the Halls of the Dead, and get stuck hanging out watching Nancy play garden gnome forever. Or maybe we'd get knocked back through our doors." His mouth was a thin, grim line. "Good for you. Not so good for me."

Cora didn't know all the circumstances of Kade's door, but she knew enough to know that he was one of the only students who had no desire to go back. While the rest of them searched, he sat back and watched, content to know that the school would be his home for the rest of his life. That was good. Someone needed to keep the lighthouse fires burning, because there would always be lost children looking for the light. It was also terrible. No one should find the place where they belonged and then reject it.

"Confection is Confection," said Rini, sounding confused. "Mom always said it was Nonsense, and then she'd laugh and kiss me and say, 'But things still do what they do, and babies still get born.'"

"So it's a Nonsense world with consistent internal rules," said Kade, sounding relieved. "You're probably near the border of Logic, or have a strong underpinning of Reason. Either way, we're not likely to get spit out unless we start trying to deny the reality around us. No one talk about nutrition."

"Wasn't planning on it," said Christopher.

Cora, who was slowly coming to realize that she was a fat girl in a world made entirely of cake—something the students at her old school would probably have called her deepest fantasy—said nothing as her cheeks flared red.

The five of them trudged along the crumble and sugar beach, moving toward the graham cracker and shortbread bedrock up ahead. Only Sumi seemed to have no trouble with the uneven ground: she was too light to sink into the sand, and walked blithely on the top of it, leaving bony footprints behind her. She was a strange double-exposure of an impossibility, rainbow skeleton and solemn black-and-white teen at the same time, and just looking at her was enough to make Cora shudder. Either of the images Sumi currently presented would have been bad. Both of them together was somehow offensive, too contradictory to be possible, too concrete to be denied.

"How far is the walk to your farm?" asked Kade.

Rini thought a moment before saying, "No more than a day. 'A good day's journey is like baking soda: use it well, and the cake will rise up to meet you.'"

Christopher blinked. "You mean the world rearranges itself so that everyplace you want to go is within a day's walk from where you are?"

"Well, sure," said Rini. "Isn't that how it works where you're from?"

"Sadly, no."

"Huh," said Rini. "And you call *my* world nonsensical."

Christopher didn't have an answer to that.

Cora's calves were aching by the time they reached the end of the beach, and it was sweet relief to step up onto the solid bedrock of baked goods, feeling them firm beneath her feet. The graham cracker and shortbread had more give to it than rock would have, like walking on the rubber-infused concrete at Disneyland. She still desperately wanted to sit down, but if all the roads here were like this one, she would be okay for a while.

They hadn't walked very far when the first of the vegetation began to appear—if you could call it that. The trees had gingerbread and fudge trunks, and spun-sugar leaves surrounding clusters of gummy fruit and jelly beans. The grass looked like it had been piped from a frosting bag. Rini paused to lean up onto her toes and grab a handful of cake pops off the lower branches of a tree, beginning to munch as she resumed walking.

"It's never a good idea to eat the ground," she said blithely, cake between her teeth and frosting on her lips. "People walk on it."

"But if the dirt here is edible, what does it matter if somebody's feet are dirty?" asked Christopher.

Rini swallowed before giving him a withering look and saying, "We still *pee*. People pee, and then other people step in it, and they walk on the ground. I don't want to eat something that has somebody's *pee* on it. That's gross. Do they eat pee where you come from?"

"It's not a given!" protested Christopher. "None of the skeletons in Mariposa do . . . that. They eat sometimes, and they still enjoy the taste of wine and ginger beer, but they don't have stomachs, so everything goes straight through them."

Cora blinked at him. "But *you*—"

"Don't ask." Christopher shook his head. "It was messy and unpleasant and we worked it out eventually, and I don't want to talk about it."

"Rini," said Kade, before she could ask Christopher to explain further, "how is it that everything here's made out of candy except for the people?"

"Oh, that's easy." Rini bit into another cake pop, swallowing before she said, "Confection is like a jawbreaker. Layers and layers and layers, all stacked on top of each other, going all the way down to the very middle, which is just this hard little ball of rock and sadness. Sort of like your world, only smaller."

"Thanks," said Kade flatly.

Rini didn't seem to notice. "It's a world, so even though nobody lived there, somebody eventually had a door that led there. She looked around, and she thought, 'Well, this is awful,' and then she thought, 'It would be better if I had some bread,' and then she found a stove and all the stuff she needed for bread, because Confection was already wanting to be born. So she baked and baked and baked. She baked all the bread she could eat, and then she baked herself a bed, and then she baked herself a house to put her bed in, and then she thought, 'Wouldn't it be nice if I had something softer to walk on,' and she baked enough bread to go all the way around the world

97

twice, so that the stone was gone, and she had a whole kingdom out of bread. It was still pretty small, though, and eventually she got bored and baked herself a doorway home, and she never came back." She paused. "But her daughter did. And her daughter didn't much care for bread, on account of how she'd been a baker's daughter all her life, but wow, did she like cookies. . . ."

Rini's story went on and on, spinning out the creation of Confection in great, lazy loops as the bakers—what seemed like an endless succession of bakers, one after the other—came through the door the Breadmaker had baked. Each of them stayed long enough to add another layer to the world, becoming the next name in the long pantheon of Confection's culinary gods.

". . . and after the Brownie-maker put down *her* layer of the world, plants started growing. I guess that's just what happens when you have that much sugar in one place."

"No," said Cora. "No, it's usually really not." She wanted to say more, like how bread got stale and moldy, and ice cream wasn't usually stable enough to serve as the basis for a glacier, no matter *how* cold it got, but she bit her tongue. The rules were different here, as they had been different in the Trenches, and in the Halls of the Dead, and in all the worlds on the other side of a disappearing, impossible door.

Rini would probably be horrified to hear

about bread mold and freezer burn and all the other things that could happen to the base materials of her world on the other side of the door. And maybe that explained the conception of Confection. Maybe the first baker, the girl who just wanted to make bread, had come from a place where there was never enough food, or where the bread went bad before she could eat it. So she'd baked and baked and baked, until her stomach wasn't empty anymore, until she wasn't afraid of starving, and then she'd gone home, having learned the only lesson that a small and empty world had to teach her.

According to Rini, Confection was like a jawbreaker. Cora thought it was more like a pearl, layers on layers on layers, all surrounding that first, all-encompassing *need*. Hunger was about as primal as needs got. What if all worlds were like that? What if they were all built up by the travelers who tripped over a doorway and found their way to someplace perfect, someplace hyperreal, someplace they could *need?* Someplace where that need could be *met?*

The beach was too far behind them now for the sound of the waves to reach, although the air still smelled faintly of strawberry. Cora supposed that could be a consequence of the soda soaked into their clothes, which was drying sweet and sticky on the skin. A fly buzzed over to investigate, its body made of a fat black jellybean, its legs strands of thinly twisted licorice. She swatted it away.

Rini, her cheeks still bulging with cake pop, stopped walking. "Uh-oh," she said, voice rendered thick and gooey by the contents of her mouth. She swallowed hard. "We have a problem."

"What is it?" asked Kade.

Rini pointed.

There, ahead, coming over a hill made of treacle tart and whipped meringue, rode what seemed like the beginnings of an army. It was impossible to tell at this distance whether their horses were real or some extremely clever bit of baking, but that didn't really matter, because a sword made of sugar can still be sharp enough to cleave all the way to the bone. The knights who rode those implacable steeds wore foiled armor that glittered in the sun, and there was no question of their intentions.

"Run, maybe?" said Rini, and turned, and fled, with the others close behind her.

Of course they tried to run: to do anything else would have been foolish.

Of course they failed. Of the five of them, only Cora ran with any regularity, and while she could be remarkably fast when she wanted to, she was more interested in endurance than in sprinting. Sumi was skeletal, lacking the large muscles that would have made it possible for her to take advantage of her light frame. Rini ran like someone who had never considered exercise to be a required part of daily life: she was slim but out of shape, and was the first to fall behind.

Kade and Christopher did the best they could, but the one was a tailor and the other had just come within a stone's throw of drowning; neither of them were very well equipped to run. In short order, they were all surrounded by armored knights on horses.

Seen up close, the horses were clearly flesh and blood, although their armor appeared to have been made from hard candy and peanut brittle, wrapped in foil to keep it from sticking to human skin or horse hair.

"Rini Onishi, you are under arrest for crimes against the Queen of Cakes," said the lead rider. Rini bared her teeth at him. He ignored her. "You will come with us."

"Well, shit," said Christopher, and that was exactly right, and there was nothing more to say.

PART III
BAKE ME A MOUNTAIN, FROST ME A SKY

7
PRISONERS OF SOMEONE ELSE'S WAR

The knights produced a surprising amount of spun-sugar rope and bound their captives, slinging them over the backs of their horses like so much dirty laundry. They seemed afraid to touch Sumi, in all her skeletal glory; in the end, they had to sling a loop of rope around her neck, like she was a dog. That seemed to be enough to make her docile: she trailed behind the slow-riding group without protest or attempt to break away.

They were all searched thoroughly before they were tied up, and anything that might be viewed as dangerous was quickly confiscated, including Rini's bracelet and Christopher's bone flute. Cora tried not to think too hard about what the loss of the bracelet could mean for the rest of them. Surely the wizard who had given it to Rini would be able to make another one, something that would let them all go back to Miss West's when this was over. Surely they weren't about to be trapped behind someone else's door, in a world that was even less right for them than the one where they'd been born. She still couldn't think of the school as "home" any more than she could consider going back to the house where her family waited for the day when she'd be cured of all the things that made her who she was, but . . .

But she couldn't stay here. This wasn't a fantasy adventure. This was a nightmare of a candy-coated wonderland, the place the kids she'd gone to school with would have expected her to dream of finding beyond an impossible door, and she wanted nothing to do with it. Nothing at all.

The riders rode, and the captives dangled, and everything began to blur together, like the landscape was accelerating around them. That was the logical nonsense of Confection coming into play, where everything was no more than a day's journey from everything else, no matter how fast you traveled or how big the world became.

(It felt a little bit like cheating—but then, to someone like Rini, airplanes and sports cars probably felt like cheating too, like a way to have all the distance in the world and not be forced to account for any of it. Cheating was always a matter of perspective, and of who was giving out the grades.)

Kade gasped. Cora twisted against her bonds as much as she could, craning her neck until she could see what he saw. Then she gasped as well, eyes going wide while she tried to take it all in.

In some ways, the castle that had appeared in front of them was nothing more nor less than a gingerbread house taken to a dramatic new extreme. It was the sort of thing children were coaxed to build at the holidays under the watchful eyes of their parents, getting flour and frosting absolutely everywhere. But true as that idea was, it didn't do justice to the towering edifice of cake and cereal brick and sugar. This was no kitchen-craft, meant to be devoured with sticky fingers after Christmas dinner. This was a monument, a landmark, an architectural marvel baked with the sole intent of standing for a thousand years.

The walls were gingerbread so dark with spice that it verged on black, hardened with molasses and strengthened with posts of twisted pretzel treats. The sugar crystals studding the walls were larger than Kade's fist, and sharpened to wicked points, until the entire structure became a weapon. The battlements looked like they had been carved from rock candy, and the towers were impossibly high, ignoring the laws of physics and common sense alike.

Rini moaned. "The castle of the Queen of Cakes," she said. "We're doomed."

"I thought your mother defeated her," hissed Cora.

"She did and she didn't," said Rini. "Once Mom died before coming back to Confection, everything started to come undone. The Queen of Cakes returned the same time the first of my fingers disappeared. *She* came back all at once, maybe because Mom killed her all at once, and she made me one ingredient at a time. I took nine months to bake. I might take nine months to disappear, one piece at a time, until all that's left is my heart, lying on the ground, beating without a body."

"Hearts don't work that way," said Christopher.

"Skeletons don't walk around," said Rini.

"All of you, silence," snapped one of the knights. "Show some respect. You're about to go before the rightful ruler of all Confection."

"There is no rightful ruler of all Confection," said Rini. "Cake and candy and fudge and gingerbread don't all follow the same rules, so how can anyone make rules that work for everyone at the same time? You follow a false queen. The First Baker would be ashamed of you. The First Oven would refuse to bake your heart. You—"

His fist caught her full in the face, snapping her head back, leaving her gasping for breath. He turned to glare at the rest of his captives, eyes resting on each of them in turn.

"Show respect, or pay the price: the choice is yours," he said, and the horses trotted on, carrying them ever closer to the castle, and to the impossible woman waiting there.

● ● ●

The main hallway of the castle continued and fulfilled the promise of its exterior: everything was candy, or cake, or some other form of baked good, but elevated to a grace and glory that would have made the bakers back home weep at the futile nature of their own efforts. Chandeliers of sugar crystals hung from the vaulted, painted chocolate ceiling. Stained sugar glass windows filtered and shattered the light, turning everything into an explosion of rainbows.

Cora could close her eyes and imagine this whole place in plastic, mass-produced for the amusement of children. That made it a little better. If she just pretended none of this was happening, that she was safe back in her bed at the school—or better, that she was sleeping in her net of kelp in the Trenches, the currents rocking her gently through her slumber—then maybe she could survive it with her sanity intact.

The jagged sugar point of the spear at her back made it a little difficult to check out completely.

Rini was limping. From the way she wobbled, it looked like her toes were starting to follow her fingers into nothingness, leaving her off-balance and unstable. Kade and Christopher were walking normally, although Christopher looked pale and a little lost. His fingers kept flexing, trying to trace chords on a flute that wasn't there anymore.

Only Sumi seemed unbothered by the change

in their situation. She plodded placidly onward, her skeletal feet clacking softly against the polished candy floor, the thin screen of her shade continuing to look around her with polite disinterest, like this was by no means a remarkable situation.

"What are they going to do to us, Rini?" asked Kade in a low voice.

"Mom said the first time she faced the Queen of Cakes, the Queen forced her to eat a *whole plate* of broccoli," said Rini.

Kade relaxed a little. "Oh, that's not so bad—"

"And then she tried to cut Mom open so she could read the future in her entrails. You can't read the future in candy entrails. They're too sticky." Rini said this in a matter-of-fact tone, like she was embarrassed to need to remind them of such a basic fact of life.

Kade paled. "See, that's bad. That's very bad."

"Silence," snapped one of the knights. They were approaching a pair of massive gingerbread doors, decorated with sheets of sugar glass in a dozen different colors. Cora frowned. They were colorful, yes, and they were beautiful, covered in tiny sugar crystals that glittered like stars in the light, but they didn't go together. None of this did. That was why she kept thinking of children playing in the kitchen: there seemed to be no sense of unity or theme in the castle. It was big. It was dramatic. It wasn't *coherent*.

This is a Nonsense world, she thought. Coherence probably wasn't a priority.

A small hatch popped open next to the door, and a pretty dancing doll sculpted from peppermint spires and taffy popped out, holding a scroll in its sticky hands.

"Her Majesty, the Unquestioned Ruler of Confection, Heir to the First Baker, the Queen of Cakes, will see you now!" proclaimed the doll. Its voice was high, shrill, and sweet, like honeyed syrup. "Be amazed at her munificence! Be delighted at her kindness! Be sure not to bite the hands that feed you!"

The doll was yanked suddenly backward, as if by a string around its waist. The hatch slammed shut, and the doors swung open, revealing the brightly colored wonderland of the throne room.

It was like Confection in miniature: a children's playroom version of the wild and potentially dangerous world outside. The walls were painted with green rolling hills topped by a pink and blue cotton candy sky. Lollipop trees and gumdrop bushes grew everywhere. The floor was polished green rock candy, like grass, like the rolling hills.

A step, and Cora saw that the walls weren't painted. They were piped frosting, puffed and placed to create the illusion of depth. Another step, and she saw that the bushes and trees were in jawbreaker pots, their roots trimmed to keep them from growing out of control.

On the third step, a veil of transplanted sugar vegetation was drawn back, and there was the Queen of Cakes, a thin, pinch-faced woman in a gown that was also a six-tiered wedding cake, its surface crafted from frosting and edible jewels. It didn't look like it could possibly be comfortable. Cora wasn't even sure the woman could move without cracking her couture and forcing it to be re-baked. She was holding a scepter in one hand, a long, elaborate stick of blown sugar and filigreed fondant, matching the crown upon her head.

The Queen looked at each of them in turn, eyes lingering for a moment on Sumi before finally settling on Rini. She smiled, slow and sweet.

"At last," she said. "Your mother did not invite me to your first birthday party, you know, and I the ruler of these lands. The first slice of cake should have been mine, to take as proper tribute."

"My mother offered the first slice of cake to the First Baker, as is right and proper, and she didn't invite *any* dead people to my party," said Rini smartly. "Not that we'd have invited you if you hadn't been dead. She always said you were the sort of person who never met a party she couldn't spoil."

The Queen of Cakes scowled for a moment— but only for a moment, her face smoothing back into pleasant placidity so fast that it felt like the scowl might well have been a lie. "Your mother was wrong about so many things. I can still remember her pouring hot grease on my hands. My beautiful hands." She held them up, showing that they were perfect and intact. "She thought to stop me, but look at me now. I'm here, healthy and hale and resuming my rule, and you, her precious little potential, you're fading away to nothing. How long do you think you have before the world realizes that you never existed and swallows you completely? I'll want to know when to plan my *own* party. The one to celebrate living forever."

"You were one of us," said Cora wonderingly.

The Queen of Cakes turned, eyes narrowed, to face her. "I don't recall inviting you to speak, *dear,*" she said. "Now shut that fat mouth of yours, or I'll fill it for you."

"You were one of us," Cora repeated, not flinching from the venom in the word "fat." If anything, it was too familiar to really hurt. She'd heard that sort of hatred before, always from the women in her Weight Watchers groups, or at Overeaters Anonymous, the ones who had starved themselves into thinness and somehow failed to find the promised land of happy acceptance that they had always been told waited for them on the other side of the scale.

"One of who?" asked the Queen, venom in every word, a poisoned slice of fudge waiting to be shoved past Cora's lips.

"You found a door. You're not *from* here any more than Sumi was." Cora glanced to Kade, looking for confirmation, and felt hot validation fill her chest when he nodded, ever so slightly telling her that his suspicions were the same. She looked back to the Queen. "Were you a baker? Sumi wasn't a baker. She was . . ."

"A violinist," said Kade. "She didn't want to bake cakes. She just wanted to do something useful with her hands. She needed Nonsense, and I guess Nonsense needed her, with you trying to make it follow rules it never wanted."

The Queen of Cakes pursed her lips. "You must be from Sumi's world," she said primly. "You're just as obnoxious as she was. She's quiet now. How did you make her that way?"

"Well, she died, so that was a large part of it," said Kade.

"Dead people normally stay in their graves, out of the way of the rest of us. This, though . . ." The Queen smiled. "What a gift you've given me. No one will ever stand against me again when they see that my great enemy has been reduced to a shadow over a skeleton. How did you achieve it? I'll let you all go home, if you'll only tell me."

It would be a lie to say that the offer wasn't, in some ways, tempting. They had each been called upon to save a world and save themselves in the process, but not *this* world. Not even Rini had been called upon to save *this* world. She was

114

trying to save her mother, which was something very different, even if it was still very admirable. They could go back to the school and wait for their doors to open, wait for the chance to go back to the worlds where things made sense, leaving this place and its nonsense behind. This wasn't their fight.

But Sumi was a silent skeleton, wreathed in shadows and rainbows, and Rini was disappearing an inch at a time, fading away according to the rules of her reality. If they left now, they couldn't save Rini. They could only leave her to be unmade, piece by piece, until there was nothing left but a memory.

(Would even that endure? If she had never been born, if she had never existed, would they remember her after she disappeared? Or would this whole madcap adventure be revised away, filed under things that never actually happened outside of a dream? What would they think had happened to Nadya, if Rini faded completely? Would they think she had found her door, gone home again, another success story for the other students to whisper about after curfew, hoping that their own doors would open now that someone else's had? Somehow, that seemed like the worst possibility of all. Nadya should be remembered for what she'd done to help them, not for what people invented to fill the space where she wasn't anymore.)

"No, thank you," said Cora primly, and she spoke for all three of them, for Kade, standing stalwart and steady, for Christopher, shaking and pale.

He didn't look well. Even Rini looked better, and she was being written out of existence.

"I didn't think you would, but I had to offer," said the Queen, leaning back in her throne. A chunk of her dress fell off and tumbled to the floor, where a butterscotch mouse with candy floss whiskers snatched it up and whisked it away. "I ask again: how is my old enemy here? What's dead is dead."

None of them said a word.

The Queen sighed. "Stubborn little children find that I can be a very cruel woman, when I want to. Did it have something to do with this?" She reached behind herself, pulling out Christopher's bone flute. "It's an odd little instrument. I blow and blow, but it doesn't make a sound."

The effect on Christopher was electric. He stood suddenly upright, vibrating, the color returning by drips to his cheeks, until they burned like he had a fever. "Give it to me," he said, and his voice was an aching whisper that somehow carried all the same.

"Oh, is this yours?" asked the Queen. "It's a funny color. What is it made of?"

"Bone." He took a jerky step forward, knees knocking. "My bone. It's *mine,* it's made of *me,* give it *back.*"

"Bone?" The Queen looked at the flute again, this time with fascinated disgust. "Liar. There's no way you could lose a bone this big and still be whole."

"The Skeleton Girl gave me another bone to replace it and it's mine you have to give it back you have to *give it back*." Christopher's voice broke into a howl on his final words, and he took off running, the rope still dangling from his neck, launching himself at the Queen of Cakes.

His hands were only a few feet from her throat when one of the knights stomped on the end of the rope, jerking him backward. Christopher slammed into the floor, landing in a heap, and began to sob.

"Fascinating," breathed the Queen. "What terrible worlds you must all come from, to think this sort of thing is normal, or should be allowed to continue. Don't worry, children. You're in Confection now. You'll be safe and happy here, and as soon as that"—she indicated Rini—"finishes fading away, you'll be able to stay forever."

She snapped her fingers.

"Guards," she said, sweetly. "Find them someplace nice to be, where I won't have to hear them screaming. And leave the skeleton here. I want to play with it."

The Queen of Cakes leaned back in her throne and smiled as her latest enemies were dragged away. What a lovely day this was shaping up to be.

8 THE TALLEST TOWER

"Someplace nice," in the castle of the Queen of Cakes, was a large, empty room with gingerbread walls and heaps of gummy fruit on the floor, presumably to serve as bedding for the prisoners. There had been no effort to chain the four of them up or keep them apart; the guards had simply dragged them up the stairs until they reached the top of what felt like the tallest tower in the world. The only window was almost too high for Cora to reach, and looking out of it revealed a rocky chocolate quarry, studded with the jagged edges of giant almonds. Oh, yes. They were stuck. Unless they could open the door, they weren't going *anywhere.*

Rini was slumped against the wall, eyes closed, the slope of one shoulder gone to whatever sucking nothingness was stealing her away one fragment at a time. Alarmingly, she wasn't the one in the worst condition. That dubious honor belonged to Christopher, who was curled into a ball next to the door, shaking uncontrollably.

"He needs his flute," said Kade, laying the back of one hand against Christopher's forehead and frowning. "He's freezing."

"Is it really made from one of his bones?" Cora dropped back to the flats of her feet and turned to face the pair.

Kade nodded grimly. "It was part of saving Mariposa, for him. He told me when I was updating the record of the world."

In addition to his duties as the school tailor, Kade was an amateur historian and mapmaker rolled into one, recording the stories of all the children who came through the school. He said it was because he was trying to accurately map the Compass that defined Nonsense and Logic, Virtue and Wickedness, all of the other cardinal directions of the worlds on the other side of their doors. Cora thought that was probably true, but she also thought he liked the excuse to talk to people about their shared differences, which became their shared similarities when held up to the right light. They had all survived something. The fact that they had survived different somethings didn't change the fact that they would always be, in certain ways, the same.

"Can it be put back?"

Christopher shook his head, and muttered weakly, "Wouldn't want it. There was something wrong inside. A dark thing. The doctors said it was a tumor. But the Skeleton Girl piped it away and freed me. Owe her . . . everything."

"But . . ."

"It's still *mine*." There was a flicker of fierceness

119

in Christopher's voice, there and gone in an instant, like it had never existed in the first place.

Kade sighed, patting Christopher on the shoulder before he rose and walked over to stand next to Cora at the window. Dropping his voice to a low murmur, he said, "This doesn't happen as much as it used to—I guess the universe figured out it was an asshole move—but it's happened before. Kids who went through doors and came back with some magical item or other that still worked in our world, where there isn't supposed to be much magic at all."

"So?"

"So you want magic in *our* world, you pretty much have to be paying for it out of your own self, somehow. Most of the time, the magic item'd been tied to the person with blood or with tears or with something else that came out of their bodies. Or, in this case, a whole damn bone. The magic that powers the flute is Christopher. If he doesn't get it back . . ."

Cora turned to gape at him, horrified. "Are you saying he'll die?"

"Maybe not die. He's never been separated from it for more than a few minutes. Maybe he'll just get really sick. Or maybe the cancer will come back. I don't *know*." Kade looked frustrated. "I interview all the newbies, I write everything down, because there are so many doors, and so many little variations on the theme, and we don't *know*. He might die if we don't get it back. He wouldn't be the first."

Their stories were written down too, by Eleanor before his time, or by the other rare scholars of travel and consequence, of the space behind the doors. They wrote about girls who wasted to nothing when they were separated from their magic shoes or golden balls, about boys who burned alive in the night when their parents took away their cooling silver bells, about children who had been found at the bottom of the garden, magically cured of some unthinkable disease, only for the sickness to come rushing back ten years later when a sibling or one of their own children broke a little crystal statue that they had been instructed not to touch.

Travel *changed* people. Not all of the changes were visible, or even logical by the rules of a world where up was always up and down was always down and skeletons stayed in the ground instead of getting up and dancing around, but that didn't make the changes go away. They existed whether they were wanted or not.

Cora, whose hair grew in naturally blue and green, all over her body, looked uneasily over her shoulder at Christopher, who was huddled in a pile of gummi bears, shivering.

"We have to get his flute back," she said.

"How do you suggest we do that?" asked Rini. Her voice was flat, dull, devoid of sparkle or whimsy. She had given up. The resignation was visible in every remaining inch of her, slumped and shattered as she was. "The Queen of Cakes has an army. We have . . . nothing. We have nothing, and she has us, and she has my mother, and it's over. We've lost. I'm going to be unborn, and then I won't have to worry about this anymore. I hope you can get away. If you can, go to the candy corn fields. The farmers there will help you hide from the Queen. She hates them and they hate her, but candy corn isn't like most crops. It won't burn. So she leaves them alone as much as she can, and you'll be okay."

Rini paused for so long that Cora thought she was done talking. Then, in a hushed tone, she said, "I'm sorry. I shouldn't have brought you here. This is all my fault."

"This is the fault of the person who killed your mother, and of the *stupid* Queen of Cakes for being all 'rar look at me I can be a despot of a magical candy world aren't I great?'" Cora kicked the wall in her frustration. The gingerbread dented inward. Not enough to offer her a way to freedom—and even if it had, the way to freedom would have involved a long, long fall. "We agreed to come because we wanted to help. We're going to help."

"How?" asked Rini. "Christopher's too sick to stand, and he's the only one of you who's been useful."

Cora opened her mouth to object, paused, and shut it with a snap. She turned to Kade. "You," she said. "You're a tailor and you write stuff down, but what did you do when you went through your door? What was on the other side?"

Kade hesitated. Then he sighed and looked out the window, and said, "Every world has its own set of criteria. Some of them are . . . pickier . . . than others. Prism is considered a Fairyland. Technically it's a Goblin Market, which means they can control where the doors manifest. Every world chooses the children who get to visit, but Prism *curates* them. Prism watches them before they sweep them up, because Prism usually keeps them. Prism is one of the worlds we mostly knew about because of the hole it made in the compass, before I went there and got myself thrown out."

Cora said nothing. Speaking would have broken the spell, would have reminded Kade that he was talking to an audience. He might have stopped then. She didn't want that.

"In Prism, the Fairy Court has been fighting a war against the Goblin Empire for thousands of years. They could have won a hundred times. So could the goblins. They don't, because the war is all they know anymore. They have so many rituals and ceremonies and traditions wrapped up in fighting that if you took their war away, they'd be lost. I didn't know that, of course. I just knew that I was going to have an adventure. That I was going to be a hero, a savior, and do something that mattered for a change."

Kade's face darkened. "The Fairy Court always snatched little girls. The prettiest little girls they could find, the ones with ribbons in their hair and lace on their dresses. They liked the contrast we made against the goblin armies."

Cora jumped a little at the word "we." "What—"

"Oh, come on." Kade gave her a half-amused sidelong look. "You said Nadya was your best friend. There's no way she didn't tell you that."

"I . . . but, yes, but . . . I . . ." Cora stopped. "I don't have the vocabulary for this."

"Most people don't, until they need it, and then they need the whole thing at once," said Kade. "My parents thought I was a girl. The people in Prism responsible for choosing their next expendable savior thought I was a girl. Hell, *I* thought I was a girl, because I'd never had the time to stop and think about why I wasn't. It took me years of saving a world that stopped wanting me when I changed my pronouns to figure it out."

"But you saved the world," said Cora.

Kade nodded. "I did. The Goblin King made me his heir when I killed him. He called me the Goblin Prince in Waiting, and that was when I realized how long I'd been waiting for someone to *see* me, to really understand who I was, under the curls and the glitter and the things I didn't want but couldn't refuse."

"So you know how to use a sword," said Cora.

"Yes." Kade paused, looking at her warily. "Why?"

Cora smiled.

The first step was moving Christopher into the middle of the room, where he'd be easily visible from the door. Getting something heavy was the second. In the end, Cora had licked her fingers and driven them over and over again into the hard-packed frosting between the baked bricks of the wall, eroding it until she'd been able to punch one of the bricks clean out. After that, it had been easy to pry another one free, jagged edges and all.

Now, she rushed the door and beat her fists against it, shouting, "Hey! Hey! We need Christopher's flute! Hey! We need *help!*"

She kept hitting, kept yelling, until her hands hurt and her throat was sore. The door might be made of hardened shortbread, but the key word there was "hardened": it was still enough to hurt her. Still, she kept going. The plan only worked if she kept going.

Eventually, as she had hoped, footsteps echoed up the stairs outside, and a voice shouted, "You! Stop that! Be quiet!"

Cora was very good at ignoring people who told her to do foolish things. She kept hitting the door and yelling.

The door slammed open without warning,

hitting her in the nose and knocking her back several feet into the tower room. That was fine. It hurt, but she had been anticipating a little pain, and she was an athlete. She was used to mashing her nose against the side of the pool, to skinning her knees and scraping her fingers. She staggered to her feet, trying to look cowed without looking overly terrified.

"We need Christopher's flute," she whined. "He's dying. Look." She pointed at Christopher, who was performing his part in their little play with distressing ease. All he had to do was lie there and look terrible. He was doing both, and they hadn't even needed to ask.

The guard at the door frowned dourly and took a step into the room, past the threshold. Cora moved fast, slamming into his side and bearing him away from the doorway. Kade, who had been hidden by the angle of the door itself while it was open, stepped forward and slammed his chunk of edible masonry as hard as he could into the back of the guard's head. The man made a gagging noise and fell down.

Rini, who had been slumped against the wall, was suddenly there, back on her feet to deliver a solid kick to the fallen guard's throat. He made another gagging noise but didn't raise his hands to protect himself.

"You should go," she said, eyes on the man's still form. "I can watch him while you go."

"By 'watch him,' do you mean—"

Rini raised her head, candy corn irises seeming even brighter and more impossible than they had back at the school. "He doesn't want to be here," she said. "The world is reordering itself so the Queen of Cakes was always, and my family was never. But there isn't supposed to be a Queen of Cakes, which means he's supposed to be someplace other than here. I'm going to tie him up, and then I'm going to find out whether he knows where he's supposed to have been this whole time. But you should take his armor first."

Kade nodded uncertainly and began stripping the man's armor away. It was gilded foil over hard chocolate: it should have melted from the heat of the guard's skin, if nothing else, but it was still fresh and sound. Cora wrinkled her nose. Some things seemed like a misuse of magic, and this was one of them.

Christopher hadn't moved throughout the commotion. She turned and knelt next to him, checking his throat for a pulse. It was there. He wasn't gone yet. He might be going, but he wasn't gone.

"We're going to get your flute," she said softly. "It's going to be okay. You'll see. Just hang on. This would be a *stupid* way to die."

Christopher didn't say anything.

When she stood, Kade was dressed in the

guard's gilded-foil armor, and was studying the guard's sword.

"It's weighted differently than I'm used to," he said. "I think it's toffee under the chocolate. But it's got an edge on it. I can make this work."

"Good," said Cora. "Let's go save the day."

9 DANCING WITH THE QUEEN OF CAKES

Kade marched Cora into the throne room, one hand clenching her shoulder so hard that it verged on painful, the stolen sword sheathed at his hip. The Queen of Cakes, sitting on her throne with her chin propped on her hand, sat up a little straighter, seeming torn between irritation at the intrusion and relief that she had something to be annoyed about.

"What are *you* doing here?" she demanded. "I didn't call for any of the prisoners to attend on me."

Sumi was tethered to the base of the throne, a braided licorice rope around her skeletal throat, and the sight of her was enough to put steel in Cora's spine. They couldn't afford to get this wrong. If they did, then this would become the reality in Confection: a woman who thought that torturing the dead was appropriate and just.

"I asked to come," said Cora quickly, before Kade could have been expected to speak. "I wanted . . . I wanted to talk to you." She thought of Rini standing naked in the turtle pond, proudly telling Nadya that her vagina was a nice one, and felt the hot red flush rise in her cheeks. Being easily embarrassed could be a weapon, if she was willing to use it that way. "I thought maybe you could . . . I thought we might have something in common."

The Queen of Cakes raked her eyes up one side of Cora and down the other. Cora, who had endured many such inspections over the years, forced herself to stand perfectly still, not flinching away. She knew what the queen was seeing. Double chin and bulging waistline and thighs that pressed against the fabric of her jeans, wearing them out a little more every day. She knew what the queen *wasn't* seeing just as well. She wasn't seeing the athlete or the scholar or the friend or the hero of the Trenches. All she was seeing was fatty fatty fat fat, because that was all they ever saw when they looked at her that way. That was all that they were looking for.

The Queen of Cakes sighed, her face softening. "Oh, you poor child," she said. "How cruel this place must seem to you. The temptation of it all—unless that's what drew you to Confection? Are you looking to eat yourself to death on the hills and leave your body where no one will ever find it?"

"No," said Cora. "I wasn't drawn to Confection. I came to help Rini get her mother back. I didn't understand what Sumi had done to this place. We were wrong."

The Queen of Cakes narrowed her eyes. "Go on," she said.

"This wasn't Sumi's world, and that means it isn't really Rini's, either. They're too . . . I don't know. Too illogical to take care of a place like this. A place like this needs a firm hand. Someone who understands willpower and discipline." She needed to be careful not to lay things on too thickly. Overselling it would lead to suspicion, and suspicion would ruin everything.

The Queen of Cakes started to smile and nod. "Yes, exactly," she said. "This place was a mess when I found my own door."

"I can believe it," lied Cora, fighting the urge to remind the Queen that she had already tried to have this conversation. When people wanted to think that they knew more than she did, she found that it was generally best to let them. "You seem so perfect for what you are. This world must have needed you very badly."

"It did," said the Queen. She leaned back in her throne. A chunk fell off of her dress and tumbled to the floor. "It called me here to bake cookies—cookies! Who wants to put more cookies into the world? No one needs that sort of disgusting extravagance. It wanted to make me fat and lazy and awful, like all the people who came before me. Well, what *I* wanted was bigger, and better, and I won, didn't I? I won. What do *you* want, little renegade?"

"I want to learn to be . . ." Cora looked at the Queen's trim waist, wreathed as it was in cake, and swallowed bile at the hypocrisy of what she was about to say. *For Christopher,* she thought, before saying, "I want to be like you."

"Bring her closer," said the Queen. "I want to see her eyes."

Kade obediently marched Cora across the room. There were two guards, one to either side of the throne, neither close enough to intervene if things went south. That was good. Both guards had a spear, in addition to their swords. That was bad. Cora took a deep breath and kept her eyes on the Queen of Cakes, trying to focus on how necessary this all was.

When they were close enough, the Queen leaned forward, gripping Cora's chin in bony fingers and tilting her head first one way, then the other.

"You could be pretty, you know," she said. "If you learned to control your appetite, if you understood how important it was to take care of yourself, you could be pretty. I've never seen hair quite like yours. Yes, you could be a striking beauty. Staying here will help you. The best way to become strong is to surround yourself with the things you can never have. The daily denial reminds you what you're suffering for."

Cora said nothing. She was used to having people assume that her size was a function of her diet, when in fact it owed more to her metabolism and her genes, neither of which she could control.

The Queen smiled. "Yes," she said, letting go of Cora's chin and sitting back in her throne. "I think I'll keep you."

"Thank you," said Cora meekly, and took a step backward, putting herself behind Kade. "Truly, you're a monarch to be emulated—and overthrown. Now!"

Kade had been trained as a hero and a warrior, and had earned the title of Goblin Prince in Waiting with his good right arm. His sword was free of its sheath before Cora finished speaking, the tip coming to rest at the hollow of the Queen's throat, pressed down just hard enough to dimple the surface of her skin.

"Don't move, now," he drawled, behind the safe shield of his helmet. "You want to hand over that flute you took from our friend? He's sorely missing it. Cora?"

"Here." She stepped forward, holding out her hand. The Queen of Cakes scowled before sullenly reaching into her dress and slapping the flute, now smeared with frosting, into Cora's palm. Cora danced back before the Queen could do anything else.

"You'll pay for this," said the Queen, in an almost-conversational tone. "I'll have your bones for gingerbread, and your candied sweetmeats for my dinner table."

"Maybe," said Kade. "Maybe not. Neither of your guards seems to be coming to save you. That tells me a lot about the kind of place you've got here." Indeed, the guards were standing frozen at their posts, seemingly unable to decide what to do next.

Cora walked over to where Sumi was tethered, leaving Kade with the Queen. Sumi turned her head to look at Cora, spectral eyes over glistening bone, and Cora suppressed her shudder. This was not the sort of thing she was prepared for.

"Hang on just a second," she said to Sumi, and walked on, stopping when she reached the first guard. "Why aren't you trying to defend your boss?"

"I don't know," said the guard. "I don't . . . None of this feels right. None of this feels real. I don't think I'm supposed to be here."

Probably because he wasn't supposed to be. He was meant to be tending a candy corn farm of his own, or fishing for some impossible catch within the waves of the Strawberry Sea. The Queen of Cakes was a dead woman as much as Sumi was, but unlike Sumi, she was dressed in skin and speech, still talking, still moving through the world. That had to warp things. For her to have a castle, she would need courtiers, and guards, and people to do the mopping-up.

"There are too many dead people here," muttered Cora. Louder, she said, "Leave, then. If

134

you're not willing to defend her, you don't have to be our enemy, and you can go. Get out and let us fix the world."

"But the Queen—"

"Really isn't going to be your main problem if you don't get the hell out." Cora bared her teeth in what might have been a smile and might have been a snarl. "Trust me. She's not going to be in a position to hand out punishments."

The guard looked at her uncertainly. Then he dropped his spear, turned, and ran for the door. He was almost there when the other guard followed suit, leaving the four of them—two truly among the living, two more than half among the dead—alone.

Cora turned and walked back to Sumi, who was still waiting with absolute patience. She dug her fingers into the braided licorice rope, feeling it squish and tear under her nails, until it gave way completely, ripping in two and setting Sumi free.

Sumi didn't seem to realize that she was free. She continued to stand where she was, shade over bone, staring straight ahead, like nothing that was happening around her genuinely mattered, or ever could. Cora wrinkled her nose before taking Sumi's hand, wrapping her fingers tight around the skeletal woman's bare bones, and leading her gently back to where Kade was holding the Queen.

"Those traitors will bake for what they've done to me," snarled the Queen of Cakes.

Kade cocked his head. "That's almost a

riddle. Will you bake them, or are you going to sentence them to some suitable length of time in your cookie factory? Not that it actually matters either way, since you're not going to be giving any orders for a while." He leaned forward and grabbed her by the arm. "Come with me."

For the first time, the Queen looked afraid. "Where—where are you taking me?"

"Where you belong," said Kade. He pulled her across the throne room to the door, shedding chunks of her dress with every step, and Cora followed, Sumi walking silently beside her, bony feet tapping on the floor.

Christopher was still breathing when they reached the tower room, and Rini had tied their captive guard up so tightly that he was more a cocoon than a captive, propped in the far corner and making muffled grunting noises against the severed gummi bear leg she had stuffed into his mouth. She raised her head when the door opened, eyes widening in relief. Well. Eye. Her left eye was gone, replaced by a patch of nothingness that somehow revealed neither the inside of her skull nor the wall behind her. It was simply gone, an absence masquerading as an abscess on the world.

"Did you . . ." She stopped herself as Sumi stepped into the room behind Cora. "Mom."

"She's still dead," spat the Queen of Cakes,

struggling against the taffy rope Kade had wrapped around her wrists. "Nothing you do is going to change that."

"I don't know," said Kade. "Killing her early seems to have brought you back just fine. Seems like cause and effect aren't all that strict around here."

He shoved the Queen of Cakes forward, until she stumbled and fell into a frosted, crumb-covered heap.

"Tie her up," he said to Rini, holding his stolen sword in front of him to ward off any possible escape attempts.

Cora stepped around him, moving toward Christopher, who looked so small, and so frail. The blood seemed to have been leeched away from his face and hands, leaving his naturally brown skin surprisingly pale, like scraped parchment stretched over a bucket of whey. She knelt, careful not to jostle him, and lifted the dead starfish of his hand off the floor.

"I think this is yours," she said, and pressed the bone flute into his hand.

Christopher opened his eyes, inhaling sharply, like it was the first true breath he'd been able to take in hours. The color came back to his skin, not all at once, but flooding outward from his hand, racing up his arm until it vanished beneath his sleeve, only to reappear as it crept up his neck and suffused his face. He sat up.

"Fuck me," he said.

"What, here? Now? In front of Kade?" Cora put on her best pretense of a simpering expression. "I'm not that kind of girl."

Christopher looked startled for a moment. Then he laughed, and stood, offering her his left hand. It was probably the only hand he was going to have free for a while. The fingers on the right were clenched so tight around the bone flute that they had gone pale again, this time from the pressure.

"Thank you," he said, with all the sincerity he had. "I don't think I had much time left."

"All part of the job," said Cora.

"Chris? You all right?" called Kade. He pressed the tip of his sword down a little harder into the hollow of the Queen's throat, dimpling the skin. "You say the word and she's gone."

The Queen said nothing, frozen in her terror while Rini wrapped more and more pulled taffy and gummy candy around her. She looked like all of this had suddenly become genuinely, awfully real, like it had all been a game to her before.

And maybe it had been, once. Maybe she had stumbled through her door into a world full of people who grew candy corn from the chocolate and graham soil and thought that none of them were real people; like none of them truly mattered. Maybe she had played at becoming despot instead of baker because she hadn't believed that there would be consequences. Not until another traveler came along, a fighter rather than a crafter, because Confection hadn't needed another baker, not with their last one sitting on a throne and demanding tribute. Not until her death at Sumi's hands . . . but even that had been reversed, forgiven by the world when Sumi died before she could return and start a proper revolution.

Until this moment, even into death and out of it again, the Queen of Cakes hadn't truly believed that she could die.

"I'd say something about being the better man, but fuck, man, I don't know," said Christopher. He stretched before slumping forward and groaning. "I feel like I've been dragged behind a truck for the last hundred miles. This is the worst. Let's never come here again."

"Deal," said Cora.

Christopher looked at Kade and the Queen of Cakes, and the room went slowly still. He took a step forward.

"I never got offered a door to this place," he said. "I'm not a baker, and I wouldn't have liked it here. Too sweet for me. Too much light, not enough crypts. I like my sugar in skull form, and my illumination to come from lanterns hung in the branches of leafless trees. This place isn't mine. But the place I *did* go, the place that *is* mine, it sort of screwed with my ideas about life and death. It made me see that the lines aren't as clear as the living always make them out to be. The lines *blur*. And you, lady? I don't want you to be dead, because I never want to see you again."

He looked away from the shaking Queen of Cakes, focusing on Kade. "Let's get the hell out of here," he said, and turned and walked out of the room.

When the others followed, they left the Queen of Cakes and the one captive guard bound and gagged, to be found or forgotten according to the whims of fate. If the Queen had thought to order her prisoners fed, she might be rescued.

Or she might not. Whatever the outcome, it no longer mattered to the rest of them. They were moving on.

10 THE CANDY CORN FARM

"Being dead for a while really messes with your staffing," said Cora, as they emerged from the castle's kitchen door and into the wide green frosting grass fields beyond. No farmers worked here, although there were a few puffy spun-sugar sheep nipping at the ground. "I figured we'd get caught at *least* twice."

"Once was enough for me," said Kade grimly. He had shed his stolen armor, but still carried his stolen sword. There was blood on the hard candy edge, commemorating that one brief encounter, that one hard slash.

Cora turned her face away. She had never seen someone die like that before. Drowning, sure. Drowning, she knew intimately. She had pulled a few sailors to their deaths with her own two hands, when there wasn't any other way to end a conflict, when the waves and the whispering foam were the only answer. She was *good* at drowning. But this . . .

This had been a stroke, and flesh opening like the skin of an orange, and blood gushing out, blood everywhere, hot and red and essentially animal in a way that seemed entirely at odds with the candy-colored wonderland around them. The people who lived here should have bled treacle or molasses or sugar syrup, not hot red animal wetness, so vital, so unthinkable, so, well, *sticky*. Cora had only brushed against one edge of one shelf stained with the stuff, and she still felt as if she would never be clean again.

"How far from here to your farm?" asked Christopher, looking to Rini. He was holding his flute in both hands now, tracing silent arpeggios along the length of it. Cora suspected that he was never going to let it go again.

"Not far," said Rini. "It usually takes most of a day to get to the castle ruins, so Mom can show me what they look like when the sunset hits them just so, and she can tell me ghost stories until the moon mantas come out and chase us away. But it never takes more than an hour or two to get back to the edge of the fields. There's not as much that's interesting about walking home, not unless robbers attack or something, and that almost never happens."

"Nonsense worlds are a little disturbing some-times," said Christopher.

Rini beamed. "Why thank you."

Sumi's rainbow-dressed skeleton was still plodding faithfully along, neither speeding up nor slowing down, not even when she put her foot down in a hole or tripped over a protruding tree root. When that happened, she would stumble, never quite falling, recover her balance, and continue following the rest of them. It wasn't clear whether she understood where she was or what she was doing there. Even Christopher lacked the vocabulary that would allow him to ask.

"Do you know yet?" asked Cora, glancing uneasily at Rini. "What you're going to do with her? You have to do *something* with her."

"I'm going to find a way to make her be alive again, so that I can be born and the Queen of Cakes can be overthrown and everything can be the way it's supposed to be." Rini's tone was firm. "I like existing. I'm not ready to unexist just because of stupid causality. I didn't invite stupid causality to my birthday party, it doesn't get to give me any presents."

"I'm not sure causality works that way, but sure," said Kade wearily. "Let's just get to where we're going, and we'll see."

Cora said nothing, but she supposed they would. It seemed inevitable, at this point. So she, and the others, walked on.

Rini was true to her word. They had been walking no more than an hour when the land dipped, becoming a gentle slope that somehow aligned with the shape of the mountains and the curve of the land to turn a simple candy corn farm into a stunning vista.

143

The fields were a lush green paean to farming, towering stalks reaching for the sky, leaves rustling with such vegetative believability that it wasn't until Cora blinked that she realized the ears of corn topping each individual stalk were actually individual pieces of candy corn, each the length of her forearm. Their spun-sugar silk blew gently in the breeze. Everything smelled of honey and sugar, and somehow that smell was exactly appropriate, exactly right.

Beehives were set up around the edge of the field, and fat striped humbugs and butterscotch candies crawled on the outside, their forms suggesting their insect progenitors only vaguely, their wings thin sheets of toffee that turned the sunlight soft and golden.

Like the castle of the Queen of Cakes, the farmhouse and barn were both built of gingerbread, a holiday craft taken to its absolute extreme. Unlike the castle, they were perfectly symmetrical and well designed, built with an eye for function as well as form, not just to use as much edible glitter as was humanly possible. The farmhouse was low and long, stretching halfway along the edge of the far field, its windows made of the same toffee as the wings of the bees. Rini smiled when she saw it, relief suffusing her remaining features and making her look young and bright and peaceful.

"My father will know what to do," she said. "My father always knows what to do."

Kade and Cora exchanged a glance. Neither of them contradicted her. If she wanted to believe that her father was an all-knowing sage who would solve everything, who were they to argue? Besides, this wasn't their world. For all they knew, she was right.

"Come on, Mom!" said Rini, exhorting Sumi to follow her into the candy corn field. "Dad's waiting!" She plunged into the green. The skeleton followed more sedately after, with the three visitors from another world bringing up the rear.

"I always thought that if I found another door, to *anywhere,* I'd take it, because anywhere had to be better than the world where my parents were asking me awful questions all the time," said Christopher. "There was this telenovela about a bunch of sick kids in a hospital that my mother made me watch like, two whole seasons of after I got back, giving me these hopeful little looks after every episode, like I was finally going to confess that yes, the Skeleton Girl was another patient with an eating disorder, or a homeless girl, or something, and not, you know, a fucking *skeleton.*"

"Let's be fair here," said Kade. "If my son came back from a journey to a magical land and told me straight up that he wanted to marry a woman who didn't have any internal organs, I'd probably spend some time trying to find a way to spin it so that he wasn't saying that."

"Oh, like you're attracted to girls because you think they have pretty kidneys," said Christopher.

Kade shrugged. "I like girls. Girls are beautiful. I like how they're soft and pretty and have skin and fatty deposits in all the places evolution has deemed appropriate. My favorite part, though, is how they have actual structural stability, on account of how they're not *skeletons*."

"Are all boys as weird as the two of you, or did I get really lucky?" asked Cora.

"We're teenagers in a magical land following a dead girl and a disappearing girl into a field of organic, pesticide-free candy corn," said Kade. "I think weird is a totally reasonable response to the situation. We're whistling through the graveyard to keep ourselves from totally losing our shit."

"Besides," said Christopher. "You don't choose your dates based on their internal organs, do you? Settle this."

"Sorry, but I have to side with Kade if you're dragging me into your little weirdness parade." Cora relaxed a little. This was starting to feel more like one of her walks around the school grounds with Nadya than a life-threatening quest. Maybe Rini was right, and her father would fix everything. Maybe they'd be able to go home s—

Cora stopped dead. "The bracelet."

"What?" Kade and Christopher stopped in turn, looking anxiously at her.

"We didn't get Rini's bracelet back from the

Queen of Cakes," said Cora. She shook her head, wide-eyed, feeling her chest start to tighten. "We were so worried about getting Christopher's flute that we didn't look for the bracelet. How are we going to get back to the school?"

"We'll figure it out," said Kade. "If nothing else, the Wizard she got the first set of beads from will be able to take care of us. Breathe. It's going to be okay."

Cora took a deep breath, eyeing him. "You really think so?"

"No," he said baldly. "It's never okay. But I told myself that every night when I was in Prism. I told myself that every morning when I woke up, still in Prism. And I got through. Sometimes that's all you can do. Just keep getting through until you don't have to do it anymore, however much time that takes, however difficult it is."

"That sounds . . ." Cora paused. "Actually, that sounds really nice. I'm not that good at lying to myself."

"Whereas I am a king of telling myself bullshit things I don't really believe but need to accept for the sake of everyone around me." Kade spread his arms, framing the moment. "I can make anything sound reasonable for five minutes."

"I can't," said Christopher. "I just refuse to die where the Skeleton Girl can't find me. I don't think this is the sort of world that connects to Mariposa. It's too far out of sync."

"What do you mean?" Cora started walking again, matching her step to theirs.

"You know Rini isn't the first person to come to our world—call it 'Earth,' since that's technically its name—from somewhere else, right?" Kade paused barely long enough for Cora to nod before he said, "Well, every time it's happened and we've known about it, someone's done their best to sit them down and ask a bunch of questions. Getting a baseline, getting more details for the Compass. Most of them, they have their own stories about doors. They knew someone who knew someone whose great-aunt disappeared for twenty years and came back the same age she'd been when she went away, full of stories that didn't make sense and with a king's ransom in diamonds in her pocket, or salt, or snakeskins. Currencies tend to differ a bit, world to world. And what we've found is that there are worlds *to* and worlds *from*."

"What do you mean?"

"Confection, it was made by the doors. Its rules were set by the bakers, and maybe those bakers came from Logical worlds, but what they wanted out of life was Nonsense, so they whipped themselves up a Nonsense world, one layer at a time. Half the nonsense probably comes from having so many cooks in the kitchen. Thirty people bake the same wedding cake, it doesn't matter if they're all masters of their craft, they're still going to come up with something that tastes a little funny."

Cora nodded slowly. "So this is a world *to*."

"Yes. Earth, now, we're a world *from*. When we get travelers, it's people like Rini, people who didn't have a choice, people who've been exiled, or who are looking for an old friend who came *to* a long time ago, and hasn't made it back yet, even though they said they were going to." Kade paused. "Earth isn't the only world *from*. We know of at least five, and that means there are probably more out there, too far away for us to have much crossover. Worlds *from* tend to be mixed up. A little Wicked, a little Virtuous. A little Logic, a little Nonsense. They may trend toward one or the other—I feel Earth's more Logical than Nonsensical, for example, although Aunt Eleanor doesn't always agree—but they exist to provide the doors with a place to anchor."

"All the worlds *to,* they connect to one or more of the worlds *from,*" said Christopher, picking up the thread. "So Mariposa and Prism both connect to Earth, and get travelers from there. And maybe they also connect to a few similar worlds, like how Nadya's world touches on Nancy's, and maybe they connect to another world *from,* so they can get the travelers they need without drawing too much attention. But when they connect to another world *to,* it's always one where the rules are almost the same."

"And the rules here aren't like the rules you had back in Mariposa," said Cora slowly.

Christopher nodded. "Exactly. Mariposa was Rhyme and Logic, and this place is Nonsense and Reason. I can't say whether it's Wicked or Virtuous, but that doesn't really matter for me, because Mariposa is Neutral, so it can sync to either. What it can't handle is Nonsense."

"My head hurts," said Cora.

"Welcome to the club," said Kade.

They had reached the end of the candy corn field. The trio stepped out of the green, onto the hard-packed crumble of the dirt in front of the farmhouse. It was impossible to tell what it was made of without tasting it, and Cora found that her curiosity didn't extend to licking the ground. That was good. It was useful to know that there were limits to how far she was willing to commit to this new reality. Or maybe she just didn't want to eat dirt.

There was Rini, in front of the farmhouse, with her arms around a man who was taller than she was by several inches. He must have towered over Sumi even when she was a fully grown adult woman, and not the teenage skeleton standing silently off to one side. His hair was yellow. Not blond: yellow, the color of ripe candy corn, the color of butterscotch.

"The people here are made of meat, right?" murmured Cora.

Kade glanced down at the patch of blood on his trousers and said, "Pretty damn sure."

"How do they not all die of malnutrition? How do they still have any *teeth?*"

"How did your skin not rot and fall off when you spent like, two years living in saltwater all the time?" Kade flashed her a quick, almost wry smile. "Every world gets to make its own rules. Sometimes those rules are going to be impossible. That doesn't make them any less enforceable."

Cora was silent for a moment. Finally, she said, "I want to go home."

"Don't we all?" asked Christopher mournfully, and that was that: there was nothing else to say. They walked toward Rini and her family, hoping for a miracle, hoping for a solution, while the fields of candy corn grew green all around them, reaching ever for the sun.

Rini waited until her friends—were they her friends now? Had they bonded sufficiently in adversity that they could use that label? She'd never really had friends before, she didn't know the rules—were almost upon her before letting go of her father and stepping back, letting him see them, letting *them* see *him*.

He was tall. They'd been able to see that from a distance, along with the unnatural yellow of his hair. What they hadn't been able to see was that his eyes were like Rini's, candy corn somehow transformed into an eye color, or that his hands were large and calloused from a lifetime spent working in the fields, or that his face had been tanned by the sun until he was almost as dark as his daughter, although his undertones were different, warm where hers were cool, ruddy red and peach, not amber and honey. They looked nothing alike. They looked absolutely alike.

Kade, who had known Sumi better than either of his companions, looked at Rini, and looked at her father, and saw Sumi in the differences between them, the places where she had been added to the recipe that, when properly baked, had resulted in her daughter.

"Sir," he said, with a very small bow. It seemed appropriate, somehow. "I'm Kade. It's a pleasure to meet you."

"Thank you for bringing my daughter home," said Rini's father. "She tells me you've had quite the adventure. The Queen of Cakes is back to her old tricks, is she? Well, I suppose that was the only thing that could happen in a world where my Sumi never made it back to me." He sounded less sad than simply resigned. This was the way he had always expected the world to go: snatching joy out of his hands for the sheer sake of doing it, and not because he, personally, had done anything to earn the loss. "My name is Ponder, and it's a pleasure to have you on my farm."

"This is no time for manners and moodiness,

Daddy," said Rini, with a little of her old imperiousness. Being near her father seemed to be bolstering her spirits, enough to remind her that, fading or not, she was still here; there was still time for her to fix this. "I found Mom. I found her bones in a world that didn't know how to laugh, and I found her spirit in a world that didn't know how to run, and now I need you to tell me how to find her heart, so I can stick them all back together again."

Rini smiled at her father when she finished, guilelessly bright, like he was the answer to all her prayers: like he was going to make things right again.

Ponder sighed deeply before reaching over to touch her cheek—not the one with the emptiness where her eye had been, but the one that was still whole and sound, untouched by the nothingness that was eating her up from the inside.

"I don't know, baby," he said. "I told you when you went that I didn't know. I'm just a candy corn farmer. My only part in this play was loving your mother and raising you, and I did both of them as well as I could, but that didn't make me worldly, and it didn't make me wise. It made me a man with a hero for a wife and a daughter who was going to do something great someday, and that was *all I wanted to be*. I never saved the day. I never challenged the gods. I was the person you could come home to when the quest was over, and I'd greet you with a warm fudge pie and a how was your day, and I'd never feel like I was being left out just because I was forever left behind."

Rini made a small sound, somewhere between a gasp and a sob, and covered her face with what was left of her hands.

"The Lord of the Dead said that Sumi's nonsense came home," said Christopher abruptly. "Mr. Ponder, Rini told us about the Bakers. How they come and make Confection bigger and stranger in order to do what they need to do. Do you know where the oven is? Where they bake the world?"

"Of course," said Ponder. "It's a day's journey from here."

Christopher smiled wanly. "I guess it would have to be," he said. "Can you show us the way?"

PART IV
THIS IS WHERE
WE CHANGE THE WORLD

11 SUGAR AND SPICE AND PAYING THE PRICE

Ponder had given them each a bag of provisions and an item he thought they might find useful: a small sickle for Cora, a jar of honey for Kade, something that was either a white rock or a very hard egg for Christopher. What he had given Rini was less clear, since she walked side by side with her mother's skeleton, hands empty, eyes fixed on the horizon.

Cora sidled over to her. "Are you all right?" she asked.

"My father gave us gifts because he had to, not because they're going to help us in the here and now," said Rini. "You can throw them away if you like."

"I don't know," said Cora, who had never owned a sickle before. She thought it was pretty. "Maybe it'll come in handy someday."

"Maybe," Rini agreed.

Cora frowned. "Okay, seriously. Are you all right?"

"Yes. No. I don't know. I've never been to see the Baker," said Rini. Her voice was low, even awed. "I always thought I'd do it someday,

157

maybe, when I felt brave enough, but I haven't done it yet, and I'm a little scared. What if she doesn't like me? Or what if she likes me so much that she wants me to stay with her for always, to be her kitchen companion and kept thing? I would do it. For my mother, for my world, I would do it. But I'd die a little more inside every hour of every day, until I was just a candy shell filled with shadows."

"Wait." Cora glanced at Kade and Christopher, alarmed. The boys were talking quietly as they walked, Christopher's fingers still tracing silent songs along the length of his flute. She looked back to Rini. "We're not going to see the Baker. We're going to see the oven the Baker used when she made the world. Big difference."

"Not really," said Rini. "You can't go into someone's kitchen while they're using it and not expect to see them."

Cora stared at her. "I thought you said the Baker left a long time ago."

"I said *a* Baker left a long time ago. One of them did. Lots of them did. The current Baker, though, she's only been here since I was a little girl. She came through a door and started making things, and she's been making things ever since." Rini shook her head. "I guess she's probably still here, even though the Queen of Cakes is alive again, because the Queen was never a Baker, not really, but she was supposed to be, and the world needs to be kept up if we don't want it to fall down."

"Oh sweet Neptune I am getting such a headache," muttered Cora, massaging her temple with one hand. "All right. I . . . all right. We're going to see a god. We're going to see the god of this messed-up cafeteria of a reality, and then we're going to go the hell back to the school and stay there until our own doors open. Yes. That's what we're going to do. We're going to do that."

"Cora?" called Kade. "You all right?"

"I'm fine," said Cora. "Just, you know. Coming to terms with the idea that we're about to go hassle someone who is *functionally divine* in this reality. Because that's exactly how I was planning to spend my afternoon."

"Could be worse," said Kade. "Could be the first god you were meeting."

Cora frowned. "This *is* the first god I'm meeting."

"Really? Because I assumed you were using the word to mean 'absolute arbiter of the rules of the reality I'm standing in.' Were you?" Kade cocked his head. "If you were, you've already met at least one god, and possibly two. *Probably* two. The Lord and Lady of the Dead, back in Nancy's world, remember? They didn't get those titles in an open election."

Cora blanched. "Really?"

"If you ask me, they probably got the same deal

the first Baker here did. Just a couple of confused kids who stumbled into a dead world and decided, for whatever reason, that they should stay." That, or the world refused to let them go. That could happen, too. Worlds could put down roots, winding them through the heart and drawing tighter with every breath, until "home" was an empty idea with nothing on the other side of it.

"Fuck." Cora shook her head, looking back to Rini, and to the silent, narrow shape of Sumi, wrapped in her own ghost. "I did *not* sign up for gods."

"None of us signed up for any of this," said Christopher. "I just wanted to live to see my sixteenth birthday."

"I just wanted to have an adventure," said Kade.

Sumi, voiceless, said nothing, and maybe that was for the best. She had been like Cora, a savior, a tool, someone who was called and offered a wonderful new existence in exchange for doing just one thing: saving the world. She'd done it, too, before she'd been killed too soon and had all her hard work revised away.

Nonsense was exhausting. Cora couldn't wait to get back to the school, where everything was dry and dreadful, but where things at least made sense from one moment into the next.

The road was made of sandy crushed graham

crackers, and wound its way through a pastoral landscape that would have been impressive even if it hadn't been crafted entirely from living sugar. Kade paused to pick a handful of sugar buttons off a bush, and munched idly as he walked.

Cora frowned. "Rini," she said. "If the Bakers made the world and then went home, where did the people come from? Like your father? I mean, he's clearly enough like the people from my world for Sumi to marry him and have you, but that doesn't make *sense,* not really. Everything else is sugar."

"Oh, there were people who didn't want to be where they were, and the world was getting so big that the Baker was spending all her time— we had the First Confectioner then, and she was *very* busy doing sugar work—fixing things. So she opened all the doors she could, and told the people who were scared or hungry or lonely or bored that if they came through, they'd never be able to go back, because the doors wouldn't open for them, but that she could give them candy hearts to make them a part of this world, and then they could stay here and be happy and fix all the things she didn't want to fix, forever." Rini shrugged. "A lot of people came, I guess. She made them new hearts, and they found places to be, and they made homes and planted fields and built ships, and now there's me, and my father has a candy heart and my mother had a meat one, and they both loved me just as much as the moon loves the sky."

"The Pied Piper of Hamelin," said Christopher, almost wonderingly.

Cora, who had never considered that there might be less personal doors, doors that swallowed entire populations whole—with or without their consent—chewed anxiously on her lip, and kept walking. She was getting *tired* of walking. It had never been one of her top ten ways to exercise. It might not even be top twenty, although she wasn't sure there *were* twenty ways to exercise worth considering, unless she started counting every swim stroke and every dance style as a different category. Worse yet, this was *necessary* walking. She couldn't complain if she wanted to.

(And even though she wanted to, she never *wanted* to. If the fat person was the first one to say "hey, I'm tired" or "hey, I'm hungry" or "hey, can we sit down," it was always because they were fat, and not because they were a human being with a flesh body that sometimes had needs. Maybe Christopher had the right of it, going someplace where people had figured out how to do without the fleshy bits, where they would be judged on their own merits, not on the things people assumed about them.)

Christopher stopped, putting one hand up before bending forward and resting both hands on his knees, flute jutting out at a jaunty angle. "Just a second," he said. "Almost died a few hours ago. Need to catch my breath."

"It's okay," said Cora magnanimously. She kicked her left foot back and reached down to grab it, pulling it up into a stretch. The muscles in her thigh protested before they relaxed, letting her work out the incipient knots.

When she glanced up again, Kade was looking at her, impressed.

"You're more flexible than I am," he said.

"Swimmer," she said. "I have to be."

Kade nodded. "Makes sense."

Rini turned and glowered at the three of them. It was an odd expression, with her one remaining eye and her half-faded cheek muscles, but she managed it all the same. "We need to keep moving," she said. "I'm running out of time."

"Sorry," said Christopher. He straightened. "I'm okay."

"Good," snapped Rini. She started walking again, and the others hurried to keep up with her.

Kade moved to walk on her left side, sparing only a brief glance for Sumi, walking on her right. He focused on Rini's face, trying not to look away from what wasn't there anymore. She deserved more than that. She deserved at least the pretense of her dignity.

"I know you can't say for sure how much farther, but we'll be there soon," he said. "The Baker will

163

help us, and then you can go home to your family, and things will be better. You'll see."

"Time kept happening here and it didn't happen for you. I'm later than you. My mother's younger than I am," said Rini bitterly. "If we fix her, does that fix *me?* Or do I keep fading, since now she's too young to be anything but a child bride for my father—and he'd never do that, he would never have *done* that, even before he had a daughter of his own. Even if we get her back and she's this much younger than me, do I still lose everything?"

"The prophecy—"

"Only said that she'd defeat the Queen of Cakes and usher in an era of peace and peanut butter cookies. It didn't say *when* she would do it, or that she'd for sure get to marry her true love and have a ravishingly beautiful daughter named Rini who'd get to grow up and find a true love of her own." Rini's mouth twisted in a bitter line. "Nobody promised me a happy ending. They didn't even promise me a happy existence."

Kade looked at the road. "We'll fix this," he said again.

"We'll try," said Rini.

They kept walking. One moment, they were passing through the pastoral fields of green frosting and sugar flowers; the next, they were approaching the gates of what looked very much like a junkyard, if junkyards were made of the

164

discarded remains of a thousand kitchen projects. Fallen soufflés, pieces of trimmed-off cake, and slabs of cracked fudge were everywhere, heaped into mountains of discarded treats behind a chain link fence of braided fruit vines. Kade blinked.

"This where we're going?" he asked.

Rini nodded, expression almost reverent. "The Baker is here," she breathed.

The four of them walked toward the gate. It swung open at their approach, and silently, they stepped inside.

The junkyard was impossibly large, stretching on toward forever, like it had its own laws about things like geometry and physics and the way the land should bend. The four travelers walked close together, their hands occasionally touching, like they were afraid that even a moment's separation might result in one or more of them disappearing into those towering piles of debris and never being seen again.

As they walked, the piles grew fresher. There was no mold—things didn't even seem to go truly stale—but there was a scent to fresh-baked goods that was missing from the heaps around the edge, a homey mixture of heat and sugar and comfort food that promised safety, security, and sweetness on the tongue.

They turned a corner, and there she was. The Baker.

She was short, and round, and had skin a few shades darker than Christopher's, and a pretty blue cloth wrapped around her head, concealing her hair. She looked no more than seventeen. Her skirt brushed the ground as she bent to remove a pie from the oven in front of her. Somehow, she had constructed a free-standing kitchen in the middle of a junkyard—or maybe she had created the junkyard around her free-standing kitchen, building it one broken cookie and discarded cupcake at a time.

Rini was staring at her, open-mouthed, a tear in her eye. Sumi actually took a step forward without being prompted, and a piece of biscotti cracked under her bony foot.

The Baker looked up from her oven and smiled. "There you are," she said, turning to put her pie down on the nearby counter. Had that counter been there a moment before? Cora wasn't sure. "I was hoping you'd make it."

Rini made a stifled gasping sound and turned her face away.

The Baker stepped out of her kitchen, walking across the broken-biscuit ground toward Rini, seemingly unaware of how the cracks smoothed out under her feet, how the cookie colors brightened, how the sugar shone. She was healing her world through her mere presence—but that presence was required. She could create. She could repair. She couldn't be everywhere at once.

166

"My poor sweet girl," said the Baker, and reached for what remained of Rini's hands. "You found her. You found our Sumi, and you brought her home."

"Can you fix her?" Rini sniffled. Tears were leaking constantly from her eye, running unchecked down her cheek. "Please, can you fix her? The Lord of the Dead said her nonsense would be here. That's all we need to put her back together again. Can you?"

"Oh, my dear," said the Baker, and let go of Rini's hands. "Nonsense returns to where it's made, that's true, but it's like flour in the air: you can't just pull it back. You have to let it settle. It goes back into everything. It makes the world continue turning. If your mother's nonsense is here, I can't reclaim it."

"Well, can you make more?" asked Cora. "You're the Baker. You're the one who makes this world what it is. Can't you just . . . whip up a new batch of nonsense?"

"It's not like gingersnaps," said the Baker.

"So it *is* like flour and it's *not* like gingersnaps and you're still the person in charge of this whole world, so why can't you just decide that what you're baking now is a happy ending for everyone involved?" Cora folded her arms, resisting the urge to scowl. "I'm tired, I'm confused, and I'm not made for a Nonsense world, so I'd be really pleased if you'd just fix it."

"Sometimes you say 'nonsense' like it's an idea and sometimes you say it like it's a proper name," said the Baker. "Why is that?"

"You found a door," said Kade.

The Baker turned to him, blinking. He shrugged.

"Maybe it was in the back of the pantry, or maybe it was in your bedroom, or heck, maybe it was in the middle of the street, but you found a door, and when you went through it, everything was different. You had a kitchen, and all the supplies you could want, and a world that wanted you to bake it a future."

"I do that literally," murmured the Baker. "The prophecies that make the future run the way it should? I pipe them onto sugar cookies and toss them to the wind for distribution. It takes a lot of time. Frosting isn't a good medium for lengthy dissertations on fate."

"I guess it wouldn't be," said Kade. "But you found a door, and it brought you here, and you know you're not the first person to work in this kitchen, so I'm guessing you're afraid that the door will come back one day and send you back to wherever you came from."

"Brooklyn," said the Baker, and just like that, she wasn't a god, or a creator figure, or anything of the sort: she was a teenager in a hijab, with flour on her hands and a downcast expression on her face. "How did you know that? Are you here to take me back?"

"We'd never do that to anyone," said Cora. "Ever. But you asked why we talk the way we do."

"If your door ever reappears, if you ever find yourself back in a world that you don't want any part of, look up Eleanor West's Home for Wayward Children, and see if you can get your parents to send you there," said Christopher. "You'll be with people who understand."

The Baker frowned. "Right," she said finally. "But that's not going to happen, because I'm going to stay here forever."

Cora and Christopher, who both knew better, exchanged a look, and said nothing. There was nothing appropriate to say.

"That's lovely for you, miss, but we'd like to get back to school and back to the business of looking for our own doors," said Kade politely. "Can't you whip up a new batch of nonsense for Sumi, so we can put her all the way back together?"

"I don't know *how,*" said the Baker, sounding frustrated. "Nonsense happens on its own. It's in the air, the water—the ground."

"Which is made of graham crackers," said Cora.

"Exactly! It makes no sense, so it makes more nonsense. I can't just whip up a batch of something that doesn't have a recipe."

"Can't you improvise?" Cora shook her head.

"Please. We've come so far, and we've already paid for this. Sumi needs help. Sumi needs a miracle. Right now, you're the one who makes the miracles. So please."

The Baker looked to each of them in turn, finally stopping on Rini, who was still weeping, even as she seemed less and less tethered to the world.

"All right," she said. "I'll try."

When the Baker had beckoned to Sumi, Sumi had gone willingly. How could she do anything else? This was the divinity of her chosen world calling her home, and even as a combination of skeleton and shade, she knew where she belonged.

Kade had helped the Baker lift Sumi up onto a long metal table that looked, if seen from the right angle, disturbingly like the autopsy table that used to occupy the basement, the one where a girl named Jack had slept and dreamed of a world defined by blood and thunder. Then he had stepped back, along with the others, and watched as she got to work.

The kitchen had no walls, and no pantry. When she needed something, she would step outside its bounds and reach down into the junkyard surrounding, coming up over and over again with the right ingredients in her hands. Eggs, milk, flour, butter, vanilla beans and ginger roots, they were all there, waiting for her to scavenge them

out of the dust. She didn't seem to understand that this was strange, that when the rest of them looked at the junkyard, they saw only failures, not the building blocks of new successes. This wasn't their place. There was no question that it was hers.

Bit by bit, she had built up Sumi's limbs with rice cereal mixed with melted marshmallow and honey, covering each layer with a thin sheet of modeling chocolate, until the combined confection began to look like human musculature. She was working on Sumi's shoulders when the timer dinged on one of her ovens. She crossed to it, opened it, and withdrew a sheet of sugar cookie organs, each dusted with a different color of sugar.

"It helps that bones don't melt," she said, using a spatula to slide the organs off the cookie sheet and onto a cooling rack. "I don't need to worry about putting something hot on top of them and losing the whole structure. That happens with the volcanos around here sometimes. It's really tedious."

"Um," said Christopher. "All of this is cool to watch, if a little nightmare fuel-esque, but people are usually made of meat, not Rice Krispy treats. We need a functional Sumi. You're making a cake that looks sort of like her."

"Baking something transforms it, and anyone who's ever eaten a piece of cake will tell you that sometimes we can take baked goods and turn them into a part of ourselves," said the Baker serenely. She was in her element: she knew exactly what she was doing, and was content to continue doing it until the job was done. "If this works, she'll be made of the same stuff as you and I."

Cora, who had heard plenty of jokes about cake and brownies going straight to her thighs, looked down at her short-clipped fingernails, picking at them to dislodge the last bits of sticky pinkness left over from the Strawberry Sea, and said nothing at all.

"Huh," said Christopher.

The Baker laughed. It was a bright, utterly joyful sound. "I love baking," she said. "It lets you make the world you want, and it makes everything delicious." She picked up a large pastry bag, beginning to pipe frosting intestines into the hollow of Sumi's gut.

Bit by bit, the glittering bone disappeared under layers of pastry. Bit by bit, the structure of the Baker's creation was built up to overlap the silent, almost disapproving shade, until the Baker was using modeling chocolate to sculpt the fine angles and planes of Sumi's face. Layers of yellow cake had been laid down for the fatty tissue, covered by a slightly thicker layer of gingerbread which was covered in turn by a fondant shell, dyed a few shades darker than Rini's skin.

"Hair, hair, hair," hummed the Baker, and leaned out of the kitchen, snatching a fistful of what looked like black candy floss out of the mess. She held it up and beamed. "You never know when you're going to need black cotton candy. Shouldn't eat the stuff, though. It'll dye your tongue black for a week." She stuck out her own tongue, which was currently a cheery shade of blue, before beginning to apply the filmy black material to the top of Sumi's head. When it was on, she picked up a roll of parchment paper and draped it delicately over the body. "She's almost ready to go into the oven. Let's hope this works."

"What happens if it doesn't?" asked Rini.

The Baker sighed. "We try something else, I suppose."

"Her skeleton will be fine," said Christopher. "I don't know whether you can bake the ghost of somebody's boring side, but the skeleton won't care unless that oven is *way* too hot."

"I'm not into cremating my cookies," said the Baker.

"There you go," said Christopher. "No worries."

The Baker laughed. "All right, I like you people. Someone come and help me lift her into the oven."

The cake, cereal, and chocolate had added so much weight to the skeleton that it took Cora and Kade working in concert to help the Baker shift the baking sheet into the oven. The heat that flowed out when she opened the door was intense enough to make them shy back, the small hairs on their arms crisping as they drew closer.

"In she goes," said the Baker, and slid the tray—and Sumi—smoothly inside. The door swung closed behind her.

"Now what?" asked Cora.

"Now we wait," said the Baker. "We wait, and we hope."

12 THE BAKER'S STORY

They sat on a broken gingerbread wall, feet dangling, sipping glasses of cool, surprisingly unmodified milk. It was sweet in the way milk was always sweet, but it wasn't malted, or chocolatey, or anything else that would have made it fit better into the world. Cora gave the Baker a curious look.

"Where did you get the milk?" she asked.

"It grows on trees," said the Baker serenely.

Cora stared.

"No, really," said the Baker. "In these big white fruits that look sort of like eggs. One of the previous bakers came up with *that*. I just enjoy it." She took another sip of her milk. "Ah. Refreshing *and* bizarre."

"Are you religious?" asked Christopher.

The Baker turned to blink at him. "Excuse me?"

"Your . . ." He waved a hand around his head. "I know that's a religious thing a lot of the time. Are you religious?"

"My family is," she said. "I think maybe I will be someday, but mostly I wear the hijab because

I enjoy not having to worry about my hair getting in the cake batter."

"Functional *and* fashionable," said Christopher, his tone an intentional mirror to hers when she had been speaking of the milk fruit. "So is it weird for you? Being a god?"

The Baker hesitated before putting her milk down. "Let's clear this up," she said. "I am *not* a god. I'm a baker. I bake things. Any magic in my food comes from the world, not from me, and I can't help it if here, my brownies are always perfect and mysteriously double as roofing materials."

"Sorry," said Christopher. "I just thought—"

"I'm not here to convert people, or to preach, or to do anything but make a lot of cookies. A continent of cookies. When I'm done, if the door opens and sends me home, I suppose I'll make cookies there."

"Do you have a name?" asked Kade.

"Layla," she said.

"Nice to meet you," he replied. "I'm Kade. These are my friends, Cora and Christopher. Rini, you already know."

Layla nodded to each of them in turn. "Nice to meet you. You all had doors of your own?"

"Goblin Prince," said Kade.

"Mermaid," said Cora.

"Beloved of the Princess of Skeletons," said Christopher.

Layla blinked. "I was with you right up until that last one."

Christopher shrugged easily. "I get that response pretty often."

Rini didn't say anything. She was miserably flicking chocolate chips from the wall, sending them clattering down into the junkyard below them. Layla sighed and leaned over to put her hand on Rini's shoulder.

"Breathe," she said.

"I think one of my lungs has stopped existing," said Rini.

"So breathe a little more shallowly," said Layla. "Just keep breathing. The baking will be done soon, and then we'll see what we'll see."

"Rini was worried," blurted Cora. Rini and Layla both turned to look at her. "About the timing. Um. If Sumi died before she was born, and we bring Sumi back to life *now* . . ."

"Oh, that's simple," said Layla. "You bring Sumi back to life now, and she returns to school with the rest of you. For us, Sumi is a grown woman, not a teenage skeleton. She'll have a few years with you before her door opens again."

"Are you the one who opens it?" asked Kade.

"No," said Layla. "I get here a year after Sumi does."

There was a momentary silence before Christopher asked, "If we're in the future—our future—right now, does that mean that if I looked you up on Facebook once I have Wi-Fi again, I'd find you, like, twelve years old and living in Brooklyn?"

"I didn't have a Facebook when I was twelve, but it doesn't matter," said Layla. "Please don't look me up. Please don't try to find me. I don't remember that happening, which means it didn't happen for me. If you change my past, my door might never open, and I might not get to bake all these cookies. I'd been waiting my whole life to bake all these cookies."

Everyone who wound up at Eleanor West's School—everyone who found a door—understood what it was to spend a lifetime waiting for something that other people wouldn't necessarily understand. Not because they were better than other people and not because they were worse, but because they had a need trapped somewhere in their bones, gnawing constantly, trying to get out.

"We won't," promised Kade.

Layla relaxed.

In the kitchen, a timer dinged. Layla stood, brushing cocoa powder off her knees and bottom, before saying, "Let's see what we've got," and starting back. The others followed, Rini walking slower and slower until she was pacing slightly behind Cora.

Cora turned to look at her quizzically. "Don't you want to see your mom?" she asked.

179

"She won't be, not yet," said Rini. "If this worked, she's not my mother today, and if it didn't, she won't be my mother tomorrow. Is it better, in Logic? Where time does the same thing every day, and runs in just one line, and your mother is always your mother, and can always wipe your tears and tell you that there, there, it's going to be all right, you are my peppermint star and my sugar syrup sea, and I'll never leave you, and I certainly won't get killed before you can even be born?"

Cora hesitated.

"Not always," she said finally, and looked away.

Rini looked relieved. "Good. I don't know if I could live with the idea that everyone else had it better and we had it worse, just because we didn't want to always do things in the same order every day."

Kade paused at the edge of the kitchen, turning and looking back over his shoulder. "Well, come on," he called, beckoning. "We need to get Sumi out of the oven before she gets burnt."

"We're coming," said Cora, and hurried, Rini beside her, up the hill.

A rush of air flowed out of the oven when Layla pulled it open, hot and sweet and smelling of brown sugar, cinnamon, and ginger. She took a step back, laughing in evident relief.

"Oh, that's a *good* smell," she said. "That's a right-and-ready smell. No charcoal or char."

"How can we help?" asked Kade.

"Grab a pair of oven mitts and lift," said Layla.

She didn't put on oven mitts before reaching into the oven: she simply grasped the metal end of the tray in her bare hands and pulled. There was no smell of burning, and she didn't make any sounds that would indicate that she was in pain. She might not do magic, but this world *was* magic, and it said that the Baker was important: the Baker would be protected.

Kade had never been very fond of cooking. Too much work for something that was too transitory. He much preferred tailoring, taking one thing and turning it into something else, something that would *last*. His parents had taken his interest in sewing after he got home from Prism as a sign that he was a little girl after all, until he'd started modifying his dresses, turning them into vests and shirts and other things that made him feel more comfortable.

He'd stuck his fingers with pins and cut himself with scissors more times than he could count. If someone had offered him a place where he could just sit and sew for a while, with all the fabric and findings he could ever want, with tools that wouldn't do him harm, no matter how careless he got, well. The temptation would be more than he could handle.

Rini hung back, unable to trust her grip with so much of her hands missing, but the others lifted as Layla ordered them, two to a side, like pallbearers preparing Sumi for her final rest. They set the tray on the baker's block at the middle of the kitchen, and Layla motioned them to step away before she reached for the sheet of parchment paper covering Sumi's face.

Cora realized she was holding her breath.

The parchment paper came away. Sumi had been gone before Cora came to the school: there was nothing there for Cora to recognize, just a beautiful, silent, teenage girl with smooth brown skin and long black hair. Her eyes were closed, lashes resting gently on her cheeks, and her mouth was a downturned bow, mercurial even when motionless.

Rini gasped before starting to cry. "Wake her up," she begged. "Please, please, wake her up."

"She needs to cool," said Layla. "If we woke her now, she'd have a fever bad enough to cook her brains and kill her all over again."

"She looks . . ." Kade reached out with one shaking hand, pulling back before he could actually brush against her skin. "She looks perfect. She looks *real*."

"Because she is real," said Layla. "The hair proves it."

"How's that?"

"If the oven hadn't wanted to put her back

together, she wouldn't have hair now." Layla beamed. "She'd have a sticky black mess attached to a bunch of melted fondant—you're not supposed to bake fondant, by the way, or frosting, or most of the other things I put onto her skeleton. Confection wanted her back, so Confection gave her back. I'm just the Baker. I put things in the oven, and the world does as it will."

It seemed like a very precise way of avoiding accusations of magic. Kade didn't say anything. Getting into an argument with someone who was helping was never a good idea, and in this case, making Layla doubt her place in Confection could result in a door and an expulsion, and then all of this would have been for nothing.

Sumi looked so real.

"Was making a new body out of candy and cake and everything enough?" asked Cora. "Will that give her back her nonsense?" Or would Sumi's quiet, solemn ghost open her new eyes and ask to be taken home—not to the school, but to the parents who believed that she was dead, the ones who'd been willing to send their daughter away when she turned out to be someone other than the good girl they had raised her to be.

"I don't know," said Layla. "I've never done this before. I don't know if anyone has."

That was a lie, but it was a necessary one. Of course someone here had done this before.

This was Confection, land of the culinary art become miracle: land of lonely children whose hands itched for pie tins or rolling pins, for the comfortable predictability of timers and sugar scoops and heaping cups of flour. This was a land where perfectly measured ingredients created nonsensical towers of whimsy and wonder—and maybe that was why they could be here, logical creatures that they were, without feeling assaulted by the world around them. Kade remembered his aunt's tales of her own Nonsense realm all too well, including the way it had turned against her once she was old enough to think as an adult did, rigidly and methodically. She would always be Nonsense-touched, but somewhere along the way, time had caught up with her enough to turn her mind against the realm that was her natural home.

Confection wasn't like that. Confection was Nonsense with rules, where baking soda would always leaven your cake and yeast would always rise. Confection could be Nonsensical *because* it had rules, and so Logical people could survive there, could even thrive there, once they had accepted that things weren't quite the same as they were in other worlds.

Layla reached over and carefully touched the first two fingers of her right hand to the curve of Sumi's remade wrist. She smiled.

"She's cool enough," she said. "We can wake her up now."

"How?" asked Christopher.

"Oh." Layla looked at him, eyes wide and surprised. "I thought you knew."

"I do," said Rini. She walked toward the table, and the others stood aside, letting her pass, until she was standing in front of Sumi, looking down at her with her sole remaining eye. She rested the back of her hand against her mother's cheek. Sumi didn't move.

"I finally had an adventure, Mama, like you're always saying I should," said Rini softly. "I went to see the Wizard of Fondant. I had to trade him two seasons of my share of the harvest, but he gave me traveling beads so I could go and bring you back. I went to the world where you were born. I breathed the air. . . ."

On and on she went, describing everything that had happened since she'd fallen out of the sky as if it were the greatest adventure the universe had ever known. How she had argued with the Queen of Turtles and bantered with the Lord of the Dead, how she had been there for the cleverest defeat of the Queen of Cakes, when a Mermaid and a Goblin Prince had conquered her at last. It was all lords and ladies and grand, noble quests, and it was magical.

Quests were a lot like dogs, Cora thought. They were much more attractive when seen from a distance, and not barking in the middle of the night or pooping all over the house. She had been there for every terrible, wearying, bone-breaking moment of this quest, and it held no magic for her. She knew it too well. But Rini described it for Sumi like it was a storybook, like it was something to whisper in a child's ear as they were drifting off to sleep, and it was beautiful. It was truly beautiful.

". . . so I need you to wake up now, Mama, and go with your friends, so you can come back here, so you can marry Papa, so I can be born." Rini leaned forward until her head was resting on Sumi's chest, closing her eye. "I want you to meet me. You always said I was the best thing you'd ever done, and I want you to meet me so you can know it's true. So wake up now, okay? Wake up, and leave, so you can come home."

"Look," whispered Kade.

Sumi's hands, which had never once in her life been still, were twitching. As the others watched, she raised them off the table and began stroking Rini's hair, her eyes still closed, her face still peaceful.

Rini sobbed and lifted her head, staring at her mother, both eyes wide and bright and filled with all the colors of a candy corn field in full harvest. Cora put her hands over her mouth to hide her gasp. Christopher grinned, and said nothing.

"Mama?" asked Rini.

Sumi opened her eyes and sat up, sending Rini stumbling back, away from the table. Sumi blinked at her. Then Sumi blinked down at her own naked, re-formed body.

"I was dead a second ago, and now I'm naked," she announced. "Do I need to be concerned?"

Kade whooped, and Christopher laughed, and Rini sobbed, and everything was different, and everything was finally the same.

PART V
WHAT CAME AFTER

13 TIME TO GO

Rini held fast to her mother's hands, squeezing until Sumi pulled away, taking a step backward.

"No and no and no again, girl who says she's a daughter of mine, in the some bright day when I get to come home, instead of coming wherever and whenever this is: don't damage the merchandise." Sumi shook her hands like she was trying to shake Rini's touch away before tucking them behind her back and shifting her sharp-eyed gaze to Layla. "The door you've baked, you're sure of where it goes?"

"I told the oven what I wanted," said Layla.

The door was gingerbread and hard candy, piped with frosting details that looked like golden filigree and dusted with a thin veneer of edible glitter. It looked like something that would open on another world. Nothing else entirely made sense.

"You're the Baker." Sumi shook her head. "Always thought you were a myth."

"When you're saving our world, I am. I come after you," said Layla, and smiled, a little shyly. She turned to look at Kade. "Remember what I said. Don't look for me. I need to find my door,

191

and that means I need everything to go just the way I remember it going. Leave me alone."

"I promise," said Kade.

"If you ever find yourself back in Brooklyn, give us a call," said Christopher. "We take students throughout the year, and it'd be nice to know that you were going to where there were familiar faces."

"I'll keep you in mind," said Layla, and flicked her hand toward the door, which swung lazily open, revealing nothing but a filmy pinkness beyond. "Now get out of here, so the timeline can stop getting tied into knots."

"Wait!" said Rini. She darted forward, pulling Sumi into a rough hug. "I love you, Mama," she whispered, before letting the younger woman go and turning away, wiping her eyes with her fully restored hand.

Sumi looked bemused. "I don't love you," she said. Rini stiffened. Sumi continued: "But I think I'm going to. See you in a few years, gumdrop."

Turning, she started for the door, with her classmates tagging after her.

The last thing Layla and Rini heard before the door swung shut behind them was Sumi asking, "So why didn't Nancy come?"

Then the door was closed, and the strangers were gone. Bit by bit, the door crumbled away, joining the debris that covered the ground. Layla looked at Rini and smiled.

"Well?" she asked. "What are you waiting for?

You have about a day's walk between here and home, and I bet your parents want to see you."

The sound Rini made was half laugh, half sob, and then she was off and running, leaving the junkyard and the girl who only wanted to make cookies behind, racing into the bright Confection hills.

Four students had left and four students returned, even if they weren't the same ones, stepping out of a door-shaped hole in the air and onto the dry brown grass of the front lawn. Eleanor was standing on the front porch, smiling wistfully— an expression that transformed into a gasp of open-mouthed delight when she saw Sumi.

"Sumi!" she cried, and started down the stairs, moving faster than such a frail-looking woman should have been able. "My darling girl, you're home!"

"Eleanor-Ely!" cried Sumi, and threw herself into Eleanor's arms, and held her tight.

Kade and Cora exchanged a glance. There would be time, soon enough, to tell Eleanor about everything that had happened: about leaving Nadya behind, about Layla, who might someday join them at the school, about the ways that Nonsense could be underpinned with Logic, and how this changed the Compass. There would be time for Kade to find Layla's family, to seize the chance to watch someone—from a distance, never interfering—who was about to be chosen by a door. There would be time for so many, many things. But for right now . . .

For right now, the only thing that mattered was an old woman and a young girl, embracing in the grass, under a bright and cloudless autumn sky.

Everything else could wait.

14 THE
DROWNED GIRL

Well. Perhaps not everything.

Nadya sat on the bank of the River of Forgotten Souls, one leg drawn up against her chest so she could rest her chin atop her knee. Turtles basked on the bank around her, their hard-shelled bodies pressing against her hip and ankle. They followed her everywhere she went, a terrapin train of devoted acolytes keeping her company in this most uncompanionable of places.

It was nice, being in the company of turtles again. The turtles back in the pond at school (which seemed more like a dream with every endless, languid day that passed here, time defined by the lapping of the water against the riverbanks, by the occasional sound of music drifting from the Hall) had never wanted to spend time with her. There wasn't enough magic in the world of her birth. Some magic worked there—Christopher's flute, or Nancy's stillness, back when she'd been a student, although Nadya had to admit that it was nothing compared to what Nancy could do here, in her natural habitat—but most magic was just too much for the local laws of nature to bear.

These turtles, though . . . these were proper, magical turtles. They didn't talk to her, not like the turtles back in Belyyreka, and the largest of them was only the size of a dinner plate, instead of being wide enough to ride upon, like her beloved Burian, who had been her steed and dearest companion in the Drowned World, but they were still willing to let her tickle their shells and stroke their long, finely pebbled necks. They let her exist among them, ever-damp and ever-weeping, and she loved them all, and she hated them all, because they were a constant reminder that what she had here was not enough. This, none of this, was enough.

"I hate everything," she said, and grabbed a stone off the bank and skipped it hard across the water, watching it hit the surface three, four, five times before it plopped and sank, joining the others she had already thrown to the bottom. Then she froze.

She had grabbed the stone with her right hand.

Nadya had been born without anything below the elbow on her right arm, a teratogenic trick of something her birthmother had been exposed to back in Mother Russia. Three mothers for Nadya: the one who bore her, the country that poisoned her, and the one who adopted her, American tourist on a misery tour of the rest of the world, well-meaning and well-intentioned and willing to take on a "special needs" child who liked nothing more than to flood the orphanage bathroom playing with the taps.

Her third mother had been the first to fit her with a prosthetic hand, which had pinched and dug into her skin and done nothing to improve her quality of life. The only things she hadn't been perfectly capable of doing with one hand were things the prosthetic didn't help her do *anyway,* lacking the fine motor control necessary to apply nail polish or thread a needle. If she'd been younger, maybe, or if she'd wanted it more, but the way it had been presented, like it was a great gift she wasn't allowed to refuse, had only served to remind her that in the eyes of her adoptive family, she would always be the poor, pitiful orphan girl with a missing hand, the one they needed to *help.*

She had never wanted that kind of help. She had only wanted to be loved. So when the waterweeds by the turtle pond had looked like a door, so open and inviting, she hadn't watched her footing on the muddy bank. She'd gotten too close. She'd tumbled in, and found herself somewhere else, somewhere that didn't want to help her. Somewhere that wanted *her* to do the helping, and promised to love her if she only would.

She had spent a lifetime in Belyyreka, and they had always called her a Drowned Girl, even when she was away from the water, and she had never considered how literal that might be, not until she had fallen into a river and felt hands yanking her by the shoulders, away from the surface, away from the real world, back into the false one, where mothers left her, one after the other, where nothing ever stayed.

In Belyyreka, she had chosen her own prosthetic, a hand made of river water, which she could decorate as she liked, with weeds and small fish and once, with a tadpole that had grown to froghood in the sheltering embrace of her palm, looking at her with a child's love before hopping away to find freedom. In Belyyreka, no one had called her broken for lacking a flesh and bone hand: they had seen it as an opportunity for her to craft a tool, a weapon, an extension of her own.

It had dissolved when that helpful neighbor had seen her floating face-down in the pond and pulled her to supposed "safety." She had thought it lost forever.

Slowly, Nadya raised her right hand to her face and stared at it, its translucent flesh, its rippling skin. There was nothing inside it. She reached down with her left hand, laying it against the surface of the water. A turtle the size of a quarter crawled into her palm. She lifted it to her water hand, sliding it through the surface. It swam a content circle before poking its head up to breathe, nostrils breaking the "skin" between the left and right knuckles.

Nadya stood. The light reflecting on the water had formed the shape of a doorway, or a grave. It was eight feet long by three feet wide, and she knew that if she dove in here, no one would come to save her. Had she really been drowning the whole time she was in Belyyreka? Had it all been a lie?

But the school was real. The school was real, and Christopher could raise the dead, and Cora's hair was like a coral reef, bright and impossible, and if magic was real, if her water hand was real, then she had only started to drown in truth when someone sought to pull her back. All she had to do was believe. All she had to do was be sure.

"We're going on a journey, little friend," she told the turtle in her palm. "Oh, I can't wait for you to meet Burian."

Nadya backed up, giving herself room for a running start before she leapt into the air, feet pointed downward like knives, set to slice through the surface of the water. She landed squarely in the middle of the dream of a door, eyes closed, hands lifted above her head, and she slid into the river without splash or ripple, and she was gone, leaving nothing but the turtles who loved her behind.

There is kindness in the world, if we know how to look for it. If we never start denying it the door.

ABOUT THE AUTHOR

Seanan lives with her cats, a vast collection of creepy dolls, and horror movies, and sufficient books to qualify her as a fire hazard.

She was the winner of the 2010 John W. Campbell Award for Best New Writer, and in 2013 she became the first person ever to appear five times on the same Hugo ballot.

Center Point Large Print
600 Brooks Road / PO Box 1
Thorndike, ME 04986-0001 USA

(207) 568-3717

US & Canada:
1 800 929-9108
www.centerpointlargeprint.com